T0374192

THE BOYS OF PEPPER BEACH

Larry Kockler

authorHOUSE®

AuthorHouse™
1663 Liberty Drive
Bloomington, IN 47403
www.authorhouse.com
Phone: 1 (800) 839-8640

This is a work of fiction. All of the characters, names, incidents,
organizations, and dialogue in this novel are either the products
of the author's imagination or are used fictitiously.

Published by AuthorHouse 08/06/2018

ISBN: 978-1-5462-5467-6 (sc)
ISBN: 978-1-5462-5466-9 (e)

Library of Congress Control Number: 2018909345

Print information available on the last page.

Any people depicted in stock imagery provided by Getty Images are models,
and such images are being used for illustrative purposes only.
Certain stock imagery © Getty Images.

This book is printed on acid-free paper.

Dedication

To Devin, my favorite canoe partner and teenager, who inspired me to tell his story as well as other stories from teenage high school boys. It's tough being a teenager and not knowing what to do. It takes good decisions to get where you should be.

Table of Contents

Chapter 1

The Ride

"I'll kill you.", Sean, a 13 year old teenager, had never heard of anyone using those words to another human being before, let alone seeing someone get stabbed and drawing blood. He was about to witness this commotion in a few minutes.

He ran across the backyard to the chainlink fence, weighted down with a large jasmine vine, and peeked over the top. Perry, a boyfriend of his back neighbor, Arlene, was stumbling out the side kitchen door and down the steps, as Arlene was stabbing him with a paring knife, putting holes in his black leather jacket, drawing blood. He was throwing peeled potatoes at her to keep her away from him. She had been peeling them for dinner before her mother got home from work and had them in a colander on the table when the argument happened.

Perry, a drummer in a popular local band, stands a head taller than Arlene, about six foot, and has a copious amount of shiny black hair, which has that wind-swept look. He was the bad boy type which girls found attractive and they wanted to tame him. Arlene was no different.

His name in the band was "Ringo", because of the many rings he wore on his fingers. He confessed he had cheated on Arlene, and she, with her volatile temper, attacked him with the paring knife. He had mentioned this to her because of his guilty feelings. Too bad for him.

Perry finally made it to his Harley, and sped off, leaving behind a drop of blood on the cement driveway, an empty colander and a puff of blue-white exhaust. He never came around again.

Florida was experiencing another long hot summer. Everyone was staying inside their air conditioned homes, being lazy. Others were sitting on their condo balconies watching the ocean, drinking their ice teas or vodka mint juleps; a great drink for the sweltering southern day. Everything had slackened its pace - even in the stifling humid heat. Sean's home was cool inside, filled with the fragrances of the many lighted scented candles grandma liked having around.

Grandpa, with thinning gray hair and wire framed eye glasses, was reading the classifieds in the newspaper. His coffee cup was on a side table near the sliding glass doors in the living room where they can look into the small narrow yard, separated by an over grown jasmine vine wall of chainlink fencing between the neighbor's yard and their's.

A gopher turtle had dug a hole right on the property line under the vine. He comes out every morning around ten o'clock to eat the newly grown grass blades. Grandpa calls him "tank", because of the way he plows through the grass.

"Someday, I'm going to paint his shell yellow so I can see him better," says Grandpa.

The house shades the back yard during this early time of day. There's a whisper of a breeze ruffling the leaves on the bushes in the back yard. It was going to be a nice day for walking, or sunbathing for the tourists.

Grandpa puts his newspaper down and says, "Sean, I'm going to call this rancher who's advertising a part I need for the lawnmower in the garage."

As he gets up to retrieve his cell phone, kept in a wicker basket on the kitchen counter, he's wearing jeans and a short sleeve white shirt with a pocket. He likes pockets to put his eyeglasses in, or a pen and pad. He still has a small belly, like most retired men his age, but is still very active around the house and yard, fixing things or mowing the lawn sometimes when Sean fails to do it. Sean says this about Grandpa: "He does have energy and doesn't like to waste time."

He comes back from the kitchen holding his cell phone and says, "Sean, tell Grandma we're going to be gone for a few hours, and not to expect us for lunch."

Sean tells Grandma in the master bedroom at one end of the house, that they are leaving to look at a part for the riding mower from the classifieds.

Grandma has her white and gray hair done up with those large curlers that look like small jet engines. She's wearing her big eyeglasses with rhinestones in the corners, doing her crossword puzzle sitting in her green overstuffed recliner with her grey striped cat, Puffy, curled up in her lap. She likes the quietness of her room, and can take quick naps without distractions from the main part of the house.

Grandpa and Sean go out to the two car garage, snatching their baseball caps off the hooks by the door, and get into the five year old dark blue Ford pickup truck. It has a wide front seat which can accommodate the three of them when out riding. The garage is also his workshop. All his tools are organized and outlined in black on the peg board above the work bench. God forbid, if you don't put the tool back in its proper place. Many a time Sean had to use his tools to fix his bike, only to catch hell if he didn't return each of them back to their black outlined space.

Grandma and grandpa bought this three bedroom home in the 70's, when a developer was building along the beach area. Most of the homes are single story with white flat cement tile roofs. It's a cement stucco home painted white, with bright yellow shutters and front door.

Out front is a triple trunk palm, a cabbage palm tree near the street, and a sago palm near the garage - all very tall for having been here thirty years or more. Grandma attempted many times to grow flowers, but they kept dying because the soil is sugar sand just like the beach. The only flowers she was successful in keeping alive were the yellow lantanas, a Florida weed that grew well along the highways, and caladiums of various red hues amongst the shrubbery, and a seven foot high Borneo giant elephant ear plant by the front door. They have to duck under its huge leaves whenever they get near it.

Grandpa backs his pickup truck out of the garage and proceeds into town, across Main Street, and then under the Interstate highway, going due west on the Old Cracker Highway, a four lane road.

They pass the Mall and other shopping centers, an old brick school, and car dealerships. One dealership is flying an American flag so big that it almost touches the ground as it flutters. A journalist for the local newspaper asked the dealer if he was using the huge flag as an advertising gimmick. The dealer insisted he was just being patriotic. After all, it was an American car he was selling. Grandpa and Sean just chuckle every time they drive by. They know what he's doing. All the other car dealerships advertise by use of multi-colored pennants and strings of white lights illuminated at night.

Then they pass by the gated communities with their pink and white stucco homes with expensive cars in the driveways.

Further on, materialize the poor neighborhoods with their shabby, wood homes and grey cement block houses. Out in front of each house there's always a collection of assorted lawn chairs and mismatched car seats. The poor, when not working, like to sit and watch the traffic go by, insisting they're not being lazy - It's just cooler outside. There are no air conditioning units in their windows.

The orange groves come next, acres and acres of them, with a big ugly orange processing plant. In season, the open trailer trucks line up in the parking lot with their loads of oranges, ready to dump them onto a conveyor belt that takes them inside to be washed and sorted out. They pass by more orange groves, which are in full bloom. The fragrance is in the air from the orange blossoms. Soon the pickers will be getting ready to harvest the fruit. The workers will cut the pant legs off of the old jeans or other type of heavier pants, pull them up over their long sleeved shirts to protect their arms against the cuts the wooden thorns would do. Some wear scarves around their necks, and a bandanna or hat also. A tapered ladder is assigned for each picker to reach up through the branches more easily. They fill their gunny sacks and dump the oranges into their numbered tubs. Each picker is paid by the amount he picks. Some pick fast. It's hard work. No white American is willing to do this. It's a rare moment when you see a desperate "honky" picking. Only the immigrants or the "illegals" are willing to pick our fruit. The lower economic groups work in the orange plant, processing the oranges, cleaning and assorting them for juice or shipping.

The groves give way to the open skies, to a sea of sawgrass, which stretches as far as the eye can see. The land is flat in central Florida. Here and there you see islands of sabal palmetto palms and clusters of black and brown cattle grazing. In the distance you see the gray and white clouds building up on the horizon - a possible storm brewing. To Sean, they looked like snow capped mountains.

Finally, they get to the end of the highway and turn north onto County Line Road, a two lane road. After driving a few miles, Grandpa says, "Look for a white cow's skull on a post. It will be on my side."

Chapter 2

Skull

Sean finally sees the white skull in the distance. "There it is Grandpa", he exclaims, pointing to it. Grandpa slows down. It's a bleached cow skull on a post with a sign overhead, that reads "Skull's Ranch".

"This is it", says Grandpa. "It's almost a mile down this dirt lane to the rancher's house."

They turn into the dirt lane, raising billows of white dust. It hasn't rained in weeks, so the land is very dry. Everything on the side of the lane is covered in white sand powder. A ditch is on one side and saw-grass on the other. Sabal palmetto palms are everywhere.

"Who would ever want to live out here?", Sean asks. The white dirt lane ends at a grassy opening, with the rancher's house straight ahead. It's a low house built out of cement block with a low roofed porch across the front. You can see an old dark wooden barn in the back yard, and some more palmetto palms and saw-grass shimmering to the horizon. There are some beef cattle grazing and dark colored horses behind the barn.

The rancher is waiting for them. "Saw your white cloud when you were driving in", he says. Grandpa gets out of his truck, as swirls of white sand dust envelope him and asks the rancher, "Are you Jim Skully?"

"Yes, I am", says the rancher, wearing an old stained cowboy hat, dirty jeans and dirty shirt. He's a tall large man, unshaven, with large white sideburns and bushy eyebrows. They shake hands and after a few words are exchanged, move off to look at the cluttered machinery pieces laying about. The front and side yards are full of junk parts.

Sean gets out of the pickup truck to see what's going on. Just then, a rock comes whizzing by his head. Ducking down, he yells, "hey!", to a girl standing on the other side of the dirt driveway. "Why did you do that?" he questions.

"I'm trying to knock dragon flies off the tips of the blades of grass" she says. Then she throws a few more rocks and hits them every time. She's a good shot.

Sean thinks she looks a bit slutty, like Moonshine McSwine from the Li'l Abner comic strips he reads in the Sunday newspaper. She's also shapely, unkempt and unwashed, with her flip-flop sandals on. There is a sprinkling of freckles across the bridge of her nose, with wild red hair and emerald green eyes.

"What's your name?" she asks.

"Sean".

"Where do you go to school?"

"I go to Pepper Beach High School. And what is your name?"

"Sharon. I go to Orange Blossom High School."

She seems like a mischievous, lonely girl craving attention. Sean could understand this, living out here, so desolate.

Sharon turns around, and bends over to pick up another rock. Sean sees she's not wearing any panties. Her jeans are cut very short, showing the cheeks of her behind.

He gets excited and turns red in the face. She senses his predicament as she turns and smiles. Sean puts his hands into his pockets and tries to look dumb. She knows exactly what she's doing and Sean is not sure how to handle this, because of her looseness.

Grandpa finally returns back to the pickup truck. He thanks the rancher for showing him around. He didn't find the part for the riding lawn mower he needed. "C'mon Sean, it's time to leave." he says.

Driving back home, Grandpa says to Sean, "Remember how you asked who would want to live out here? Well, the rancher has four generations of family here. His great grandfather had come before the Civil War. Florida was important to the Confederacy, to supply its armies with cattle, hogs, salt and cotton. In the cattle drives north, the Cow Cavalry, or cowboys, as they were called, had to protect the cattle from Union raiders or Confederate deserters. The cowboys were able to stay with their families and farm, rather than being put into army battalions. It wasn't a matter of territory, but of supplying cattle to the southern armies. When the Confederacy surrendered, Florida became part of the Union. His great grandfather stayed, gathered all the wild cattle around and farmed the 2000 acres Florida gave him to home-stead. These wild cattle were brought over by the Spanish. Those that escaped, flourished. The early ranches had access to those free ranging Andalusia cattle, and eventually developed these huge beef cattle ranches, so important to the state culturally and economically."

"Wow! Grandpa, that was some history lesson. Who would have guessed? Still, I would never want to live so remotely. I like it where we are now. I have plenty to do - not like that girl throwing rocks at the bugs. I think she has no friends and is lonely. Don't get me wrong - she is cute, but I just got that feeling she preferred to ride me than a horse on her family's ranch." Grandpa just chuckles.

Chapter 3

Chase

Sean turned 15 years old this summer, and enters his freshman year in high school. Arlene, who lives behind his home, is two years older, and needs transportation to a pool party she was invited to. She had a romantic attachment to a senior boy who would be there. She was a small 5' 4" cute Italian girl with olive colored skin and short dark hair combed back over her ears, held in place with a hair band. She has dark brown eyes and wears gold hoop earrings.

Sean is slender, 5' 8" tall, with light brown hair touching his shoulders, and hazel eyes.

Arlene agrees to sit on the bike's crossbar to make the long bike ride out to the area of meadows and ranches, where the party is being held at Lance's home, a senior and captain of the high school tennis team. He is tall with long blonde hair, blue eyes, handsome and popular - a rich boy. This is his eighteenth birthday and he's celebrating while his parents are away on vacation. His father is a hay farmer, harvesting Tifton 44, a young succulent hay loaded with nutrients for horses and cows. Then the hay would be wrapped in a light green mesh and sold in round or square bales.

The house is on Soaring Hawk Lane, and sits up on a slight rise of the land, with 200 feet of sloping lawn all around it. It is a two story white clapboard house with wings on each side. One side is a two car garage and the other side a large family room with a fireplace.

In front is a two column portico covering a double set of tall wooden front doors with leaded glass inserts. Overhead is hanging a large bronze glass lantern.

The hedges in front, of various shapes and sizes, are well manicured, with tall podocarpus - a tall slender green bush - on each side of the portico. Decorative black window shutters enhanced the beauty of the home.

A low split rail fence borders the street. A wide cement driveway curves up to the house, with a parking apron in front of the garage. The property exudes wealth and taste.

Across the street are the big hay fields, as well as to the side of the house. You can see trees along the edges of these fields. There are cars parked on the driveway and along the street in front. Sean hears the music coming from the back of the house, and parks his bike on the side of the garage behind some bushes, and enters the huge screened enclosure around the pool.

Arlene was already inside, and has disappeared into the crowd. There were about 30 or 40 students standing around - mostly seniors, a few juniors, and Sean, the youngest one. He recognized a few of the guys from high school.

The girls were all wearing two piece bathing suits, and the guys, swim trunks. Music was coming out of a jukebox. So "cool" he thought. A long table with a white tablecloth was against the wall of the house, and loaded with finger food. Two Spanish speaking maids, scurrying around, kept the table supplied with food, and were picking up the discarded plates and cups.

At each end of the table, was a big bowl of salsa and chips. Huge trays were filled with small cut sandwiches, and pigs in a blanket ready to pick up and eat. There was another tray of fruit and cheese. Watermelon and cantaloupes were cut into narrow wedges and weren't drippy when eaten. Plenty of colored plastic cups, plates and napkins were around. "What a spread," he thought.

He noticed a large pitcher with a sign taped to it saying "mimos". - Found out later, that meant mimosas, a chilled drink of orange juice and champagne. Sean was not surprised to find tubs of iced beer and sodas. He knew teenagers drank this stuff at their gatherings.

On the other side of the pool enclosure was a pool house. He enters without making a sound, observing a billiard table at one end, with a couple making out on the rattan furniture at the other end. Along the back wall were arcade machines to play and a picture of Lance with his tennis racquet in hand.

He changed into his swim trunks in the bathroom and took his backpack to his bicycle on the side of the garage.

Returning back to the pool area, a girl came over and asked him to write his name on a piece of paper and put it into a bowl she was carrying, for a swimming event coming up.

It was announced later that it was time to play the game. You draw a name from the bowl, swim to the bottom of the pool, kiss your girl for five minutes and then swim back up.

Sean drew a name of a senior girl he did not know, and swam to the bottom of the pool. She grabs him and shocks him by sticking her tongue in his mouth. He gasps for air, taking water instead, causing him to cough as he reached the top of the water. One big senior dude, with a tattoo on his muscular arm, pulls Sean out of the water.

"Are you okay bro?"

"Yah, I wasn't expecting her to put her tongue in my mouth. It caught me off guard."

"She does that to all the guys. She likes French kissing, so be careful - she's a wild one."

Sean is having a good time swimming and bonding with the older guys. Sometimes, they would mess up his long, wet hair, or give him a head lock with a knuckle rub across his scalp. He loved every minute of it, feeling like their little brother, with all the attention being bestowed upon him.

The guys all talked about the girls, and the girls talked about the guys, huddled in groups along the pool edge, with their feet dangling in the water.

It was getting late, and the crowd was starting to thin out. He figured it was time to leave. Changing into his street clothes, he searches for Arlene, who wasn't around the pool area anymore. He walks down to the big pole barn at the other end of the property, hoping she might be there. Lance and two of his buddies were on top of the hay, drinking beer.

"Hey, what ya doing?" one of them yells down.

"I'm looking for Arlene so we can go home." he yells back.

"What's your name?" one guy asks.

"Sean".

"You're cute. Can we see your dick?"

"What? NO!" he said.

They started to slide down from the hay. "C'mon, show us your dick."

He knew they were drinking so he started to move away, not liking what they were implying.

"Are you going to leave us?" one of them asked as he was stumbling from drinking too much beer.

"See ya", Sean said.

They were bigger and stronger than him. He got scared and started to run. They blocked him no matter which direction he ran. Soon they had him heading into the woods, howling and yelling "We're going to get you! We're going to get ya!"

Sean ran as fast as he could through the trees, going deeper and deeper into the woods, feeling like a trapped lamb being chased by howling wolves on each side. Finally, one of them tripped him up, and down he goes. They were quick, and on top of him before he could escape.

"We have you now little guy," Lance said drunkenly. Fighting back as hard as he could, Sean was no match against them. His arms were pinned down and Lance had him by the legs. The guy with the dark hair pulled the shirt off and held the arms over Sean's head. Lance pulled off the sneakers, the short pants and underwear.

Sean was screaming "Stop! Stop! Don't do this!" He was so terrified.

"No one can hear you in the woods." someone said.

Lance and his other friend Casper brought his legs up over his chest. He could hardly breathe. He felt so helpless, screaming again "God will get you! God will get you!"

They just laughed. He knew what they were going to do, again begging "Please, please don't do this!"

The guy with the dark hair stuffed the underwear in his mouth to muffle the sounds.

Lance has taken his pants down, has a lecherous look on his face; while Casper, the smaller guy with light brown hair, just watched, rubbing his cold beer can across his forehead. He looked like he didn't want any part of this, but just stayed quiet and watched.

Sean looked up into the early evening sky thinking he should have gotten his shoulder length hair cut earlier, as Grandpa had resonated with the words "you look kind of girly."

When the pain got so horrible, Sean passed out.

Chapter 4

Dark Woods

Sean wakes up. Not opening his eyes, he lays there listening to the darkness. The sounds of nature can be very loud at night, louder than he ever imagined. He could hear the crickets chirping with their back legs, and hears a bit of rustling among the dry leaves. Something came over and sniffed him and then moved off. He doesn't want to know what animal it was.

Sean moved his hands and felt his body. It was cool to the touch, and naked. "Naked! What am I doing naked?" he thought. Then it came to him what had happened. "I hate them! I hate them!", he said out loud, but still didn't open his eyes.

He felt his anus, which was sore and damp. Bringing his fingers up to his nose, he smelled blood. "Those bastards left me out here to die! Ha ha! Not dead yet!", he proclaims to the night.

Every few minutes he could hear an owl hooting. This went on for some time. Then in the distance came the returned hoot from the female owl. With a raucous sound, and a flutter of wings, the male owl was gone.

The darkness finally whispers to him, "It's okay now.

You can open your eyes." Sean opens his eyes and sees only inky blackness. Through the tree leaves overhead, the stars are twinkling.

Where am I? How far did I run into the woods? Hey where is that light coming from? It seems so far away." he thinks. "Where are my shorts and underwear?"

Sweeping his hands through the leaves on the ground, he touches something. It's his shirt. Next are his shorts and underwear. He puts them on. The sneakers are nearby and they go on too. Sean laces them up. It's time to stand up. "Wow! No pain - thank God", he thinks.

It's so incredibly black, he can't even see anything in front of him. A light in the distance is coming through the trees and he starts heading for it. It's so far away. The branches are lashing him in the face as he pushes through them. He keeps falling and stumbling over fallen debris, and cutting his hands on things he can't see. By following the light, he breaks out of the woods near the pole barn which has a light on one of the poles.

"Damn! What a stroke of luck", he says. It's so quiet. The pole light throws off a pale blue hue. Cautiously he proceeds to Lance's garage to recover his bicycle hidden in the bushes. No one is around. The house is dark. "Arlene must have found her own way home by now", he thinks.

He reaches into his backpack and pulls out the cell phone to call Grandma, telling her he's still at the party house and not to worry as he will be home late.

"Okay", she says. "I was beginning to worry."

Sean can't sit on his bike seat too long because of the pain. He walked most of the way home holding the handlebars. It would be a long walk. Tears are running hot down his cheeks, feeling so despondent that this has happened to him.

Finally, managing to get to the beach, he strips out of his

clothes and bathes in the ocean to wash the stink of this day off him. No one is around. The underwear is tossed into the rubbish bin so Grandpa wouldn't see the blood stains at home and ask questions.

Sean sits naked in the pavilion, letting the night breezes dry him off. He couldn't stop thinking how God would let this happen to him. He was a good Catholic boy going to church every Sunday. He knew his life would be different now. He can't tell his friends what happened. They might think he's gay, which he was not. He just felt so dirty and ashamed as if it was somehow his fault for inviting it.

Chapter 5

Zack

Zack and his mother live in a mobile home park a few streets down from Sean's neighborhood. Growing up, he got picked on a lot by the bullies. They would punch and kick him while on the ground, and call him names, like fag or nerd. Other times, they would slam him into his locker and stick papers on it, saying "Loser", even giving him a black eye to take home. He didn't fight back. He didn't know how to fight. They were so much bigger and stronger than he was.

By age 14, Zack had enough. The taking of alcohol and drugs started to become his routine. This would calm him down and lessen the pain he endured daily. At his parents' parties, he stole people's drinks - it didn't matter what it was. He drank, he felt good. He even took his mother's drugs lying around. Marijuana and cocaine caused him to pass out. He failed that year in his class, only to repeat it the following year.

One night, a voice woke him up. "Zack, your pain is over. Go seek your future."

"What a revelation!" he thought. It took some time before he fell back asleep.

He asked his uncle, a teacher in the Marines, to give him some martial arts training, and teach him how to fight. He was taking vitamin drinks that summer and was starting to grow and show muscle. His uncle taught him how to "sweep kick" the legs out from under his opponents. This he practiced over and over again until he was proficient with the maneuver. This was his best defense. By the time he returned to school, it was "watch out bullies!" Zack fought with rage, taking his revenge out on anyone who offended him. He fought instantly, throwing his hat down and saying, "Let's do it!"

At Pepper Beach High School, he became the champion of the girls. You dare not insult or push them around, or else, you had to deal with Zack's wrath. He is now six feet tall, and had some weight on. He has dark hair in a buzz cut, dark eyes, and always wears a cap. He was a frequent visitor to the Principal's office for fighting.

Zack would fall in love with any girl that flirted with him, and she instantly became his girlfriend. Little gifts and bracelets, he gave them. He just couldn't keep money in his pockets. He wrote romantic "rap songs," and sang them out of tune. The girls told him he was good, so he sang some more. They were infatuated with him. He was a country boy - at least that's what he would tell everybody. "I'm not a redneck and I'm not a rebel", he would proclaim. No one dared make fun of his clothes or outfits of camouflage pants and cap in school. He'd been known to throw people down the stairs, kick them with his heavy boots, and "punch face". He did end up with a few scars from knife fights. As he healed, he would sing the song he loved, "Lord, How Long Does My Country Road Have To Be?" out of tune, of course. Zack didn't have much in the way of clothing, but he did respect what he had, and always picked up after himself. His bedroom was small, with a bunk bed, in case anyone had to stay over, and a chest of drawers. His mother had taught him how to iron his shirts, and he hung them carefully up in his closet.

This wasn't his mother's double wide mobile home that they lived in, but her boyfriend's. She never wanted to marry again, and Zack understood that.

Going to his grandparents' small ranch in Central Florida, was a big deal. He fed the chickens, chased the hogs with the tractor, and worked in the garden. His father lives on the property in an old trailer off to the side. He taught Zack how to shoot a gun and how to skin a hog or deer on a gambrel.

He loved it, especially the camp outs and having an occasional beer with the boys. Every Saturday afternoon, a small Baptist Church nearby, had youth activities and prayers. The Pastor would ask Zack to come up in front of the membership and give one of his "Christian raps". Zack would take his hat off and with hand motions, talk-sing his rap, making it up as he went along. He was devout, and believed with his whole heart in his Lord Jesus. Amen.

Chapter 6

Little Zack

Zack, as a child, was sitting up in his bed listening to his Dad and Mom arguing again. Tonight it was particularly loud. He hardly knew his Dad, but when he was around, it seemed the arguments started. His eyes were moist, on the verge of tears, as he sat there clutching his stuffed dog, Snoopy, with an elongated neck from holding him too tight as he dragged him around every where he went. It was some sort of a security blanket for him.

Then there was a long silence. He just sat there and listened. He thought he heard a thump. So he got out of bed and walked down the hallway in his blue pajamas, with lambs and white clouds on them. He headed for the lighted living room where he could see his mother laying on the floor with her back to him. She appeared to be asleep. Her arm was outstretched, pointing towards an empty liquor bottle. Red was all around her wrist. He reached out and touched her. "Mommy, Mommy". She didn't move. He got scared and shook his mother again. She still didn't move. So he went to her purse on the couch, took out her cell phone and punched in 911, as his mother had taught him so many times before to do if he felt unsafe.

"911, how can I help you?" the operator asks on the cell phone.

"My Mommy is asleep and won't wake up."

"What is your name?"

"Zack."

"How old are you Zack?"

"Five years old."

"Where is your Mommy?"

"On the floor."

"What is her name?"

"Mommy."

"Okay, I will send a policeman and ambulance for her. Will that be okay?"

"Okay."

"Can you go to the front door and open it?"

"Yes."

"I want you to stand in the light of the doorway so the policeman can see you. Soon you will see blinking red lights of his car. Stay on the telephone with me until the policeman arrives. Are you afraid?"

"No."

Soon, a police car shows up with the ambulance. The policewoman says "Are you Zack? Where is your Mommy?"

"Over there on the floor", as he points to her laying on the carpeted floor.

The policewoman says "I will stay with you as the ambulance attendants fix up your Mommy."

Zack's eyes are as big as quarters, as he watches the attendants bandage his mother's arm and put tubes in her, with bags of clear fluid flowing into her arm. Then they lifted her up and put her on a gurney and wheeled her out to the ambulance. The policewoman said they are taking her to the hospital. Meanwhile, she was searching his mother's cell phone to find some relative to come and take care of Zack. She talks to his grandparents, who said they were about a half hour ride to their daughter's place. The policewoman stayed with Zack until his grandparents arrived with hugs and kisses. Zack felt better with them around.

The next day, in the afternoon, Zack's grandparents take him to the hospital to see his Mom. She was asleep when they arrived. Slowly she wakes up and holds her good hand out to help him climb into bed with her. "How's my baby?", she said, as she gave him a big hug. He nestles in beside her with his stuffed dog, Snoopy.

As she was lying there with her son snuggled up next to her, she kept wondering why she was drinking and slashing her wrists. Just because she was lonely and unhappy, was no reason to have her son unhappy too, possibly living out his life in foster care. How selfish of her. This was the moment to take control of her life and give little Zack the upbringing he needed. This was the most important time of his life. I am his mother, and I should be doing a better job of it. I must come to terms with this.

Chapter 7

Adam

Adam was built slightly smaller than Zack and Sean. His hair was straight and blonde, and hung down over his forehead to one side. He has blue eyes. The girls in high school thought he was sooo cute. As they passed him in the hallway, they would always give him that look and smile. Some would even say, "Hi Adam." He was smart, very focused, and an honor student. He worked hard at everything he attempted. He was also the best junior varsity basketball player in high school. Some students considered him the "star of the team". Being fast and quick, darting in and out grabbing the basketball, he could play off the backboard very well. Shooting from the perimeter or laying up to the hoop, he could sink 8 out of 10 tries to score points. The girls loved it and came to every game to scream every time he scored.

When the game was over, some of the girls would gather around Adam, as he toweled the sweat off, just to get a smile or some kind of notice. He would just smile and not say anything. Every high school girl wanted to be his girlfriend, mess up his hair, and stick their tongue in his mouth. If Adam was aware of this, he sure didn't let on.

He had a slightly chubby girlfriend, as tall as him, with medium highlighted brown hair and soft brown eyes. Sheila was her name. She was an honor student like Adam, and kept up with the latest dress fashions, cosmetics and hairdos. It was said, she was an heiress or something, because she always seems to have money. She wore a small diamond on a chain around her neck.

Adam liked wearing short pants, especially the cargo pants with the big pockets on the side. His appearance was casual. He liked wearing the slip on loafers or those canvas boat shoes. A tee shirt with a button down shirt with sleeves rolled up over it, was the extent of his fashion dress. He was not a clothes hog, like Sheila, or some of the other jocks in school.

They both wrote articles for the school's monthly news bulletin called "The Sand Dollar", named for those white shells along their shoreline beaches. Sheila wrote the section "fashion for the teenage girl", and Adam contributed to the sports section. Sometimes, they would collaborate on mutual interests. They once exchanged "friendship bracelets", made from colorful yarn and plastic. Actually, she made them for both of them. Many of the girls in his class never understood their relationship. They would whisper among themselves what they thought it could be. They were all wrong, of course.

Her family owned a 42 foot inbound sports fishing cruiser with a flying bridge over the cabin. Her father would navigate the boat from up here with an all around view of the water. Occasionally she'd ask Adam to come out fishing with family and friends. Usually she wore a white one piece bathing suit with skirted bottom, pink floral eyelet slip on shoes, and floppy straw sunhat with pink nails, pink lipstick, and big white sunglasses.

She was the only girl that had touched his body, suggesting an application of suntan lotion. His skin had a youthful radiance over his lean muscular frame, developed from many months of climbing the rope and rings at gym. They were good friends. She knew this, as he showed no girlfriend interest in her at all.

On fishing trips, Adam was not squeamish in handling slimy worms to bait everyone's hooks. Sheila announced a new title to be given to Adam - the "Master Baiter". Everyone on the boat cheered. Adam turned a little red in the face, but he handled it well by thanking everyone for such an esteemed title. As he went to the gunwales, to cast his fishing line overboard, he thought, "my word is the same, but has an 'or' on the end, and I'm good at that too." Then he adjusted his cap and sunglasses, and allowed a smile to come across his face.

Chapter 8

Town

Pepper Beach got its name from the great strands of Brazilian pepper bushes mixed in the red mangroves, cabbage palms and palmetto palms, along its shoreline and waterway. The pepper bush was brought to Florida in the 1800's as a Christmas ornamental of red berries and green shiny leaves, later called Florida holly. It's very abundant and invasive, and can grow anywhere; especially in salt marsh edges. They are poison to eat, and can itch when touched. Birds love to eat them for its narcotic affect. It's also used as a peppercorn for culinary purposes.

Pepper Beach is divided by the Inter-coastal Waterway. The western side is the business area of the city. Main Street has City Hall, the Police Headquarters, Fire Department, a four story parking garage, and all the functions a city needs to run itself. The eastern side is the beach. Once you cross over the Waterway, the street becomes Beach Street. In olden days it was called "to the beach street". Beach Street goes along the causeway to the ocean. You pass the yellow condos with their barrel tiled roofs, the iron fences, and tailored hedges of ligustrum, and bright red bougainvilleas. Then you pass an open area for families cooking and drinking under the pavilions, watching their children splashing in the waterway. A jet ski business is there for rentals. Then you come into the fun part of the street, of shops tailored to the tourist and beach goers. There are restaurants with their colored awnings and sidewalk umbrella tables. A bathing suit shop with shoe wear in the window, of flip flops in any color you want. Then a little store that sells magazines, newspapers, cigars and "believe it or not" tea. Inside is a case built into the wall, lighted with all kinds of tea pots and tea holders. Jars of tea, from all over the world are on display - black tea, green tea from India, China and Southeast Asia. Grandma likes going here once a month to get her personal blends of tea. It's not cheap, so she only has one cup a day. Outside on the sidewalk are two tables and chairs. The men love sitting here away from their wives, to read their newspapers, smoke a cigar and have a cup of tea, while the wives are at the women's clothing stores.

Other shops are the Bicycle Shop, Novelties, and Sandwich Shop. The last one is a Surfer Shop, called "Ron's Surf Shop". He displays his surf boards outside on the sidewalk, and others inside. Sean likes going back into the work area to talk with the hippies with long hair. They smoke so much weed, he thinks their brains are fried. They only talk crap. The owner, Ron, called them numb skulls, because they have no brains and some of them never graduated from high school. They work cheap, polishing, grinding, and sanding the boards. As long as Ron lets them use his old boards to surf, they hang around and work for him.

Across the street is a cleaners, hair salon, patio furniture store, a small pizza store that sells by the slice, a Chinese take out, and every teenager's favorite, Mad Eddie's, a record music store with a young funky owner with wild hair and red eyeglasses. All the music nerds love its friendly atmosphere promoting music. Sean likes to spend his free time here searching for cassettes for his head phones. Tee shirts of recording artists are displayed, as well as bracelets, neck jewelry and wrist bands, in a glass case near the door. The town wants no national stores, just "Mom and Pop" businesses to keep that small town feeling.

On the beach side is Rent-A-Bike, small motel, and a convenient store with a liquor store attached. There's the Blue Tiki Restaurant with a thatch roof, serving lobster bisque, a tourist's favorite, and "Happy Hour" every afternoon. Beach Street ends at a roundabout with a big metal sculpture of a painted grouper in the middle, and low plants at the base. At night, it is lighted. The symbol of the grouper was chosen, because they are so abundant on the reefs. The fishermen do well in catching them. Some of them can get up to 200 pounds each, and are as big as a sand shark. Excursion boats will take you out for deep sea fishing, and volleyball courts are set up on the beach. The games can become intense, so be careful on the sidelines, of getting hit with the ball or a player. Other activities are para sailing, fishing off the jetty, and charter boats to rent for diving or deep sea fishing, and, of course, surfing.

The three of them meet down on the beach about mid-morning, bringing beach towels and suntan lotion. They wore baseball caps as well as sunglasses. It was a warm day and the tourists are coming down to the beach, from their condos, bringing an assemblage of umbrellas, chairs, and coolers. Zack was not impressed with the ladies he was seeing that day.

"Look at that. That fat lady's thighs and ass are as big as my whole body. What are those lumps on her legs?" he asks.

"Cellulite" Sean answers.

"What's that?"

"Lumps of fat cells that women get when overweight." He answers again.

"This is disgusting", says Zack, "Even her boobs are huge, like cantaloupes".

They all chuckle.

"I'm going further down the beach to see if there are any chicks lying around", says Zack. "Anything is better than this. See ya".

Adam and Sean are just content to lie there and take it all in. Some time goes by, and Zack hasn't returned. So, out of curiosity, they walk down the beach, finding him sitting with some girls in bikinis, all wearing those big Hollywood sunglasses, being entertained by him. Zack sees them and yells out "C'mon over and meet these nice gals". They saunter over and sit down. Zack is telling them he's a country boy, talking with a southern accent, so thick, you could cut it with a knife. "Howdy madam, yes madam, no madam", with enough "ya'll" thrown in to impress any girl from the North. They were amused, besides the fact that he was strong and handsome.

A young boy is playing with his boogie board down by the water's edge. Zack goes down to ask if he could try it. "Sure", says the boy. Zack throws the board down at the edge of the water, and with a running start, attempts to slide on the board. In three steps, he misses, and lands on his belly. The girls laugh. This doesn't bother him - he has their attention. He gives a wave, and with a few more tries, he's skimming along the water's edge. Satisfied, he comes back, flops on his towel, and says "So girls, what do ya'll think? Cool huh?"

Adam and Sean have had enough of Zack's antics.

"Zack, we're going back to our towels. We'll see ya'll later." As they walk away, Sean says to Adam, "I just had to throw in that "ya'll" for fun." Adam gives a laugh.

Pepper Beach is a great place for young people to grow up, especially the boys, dashing about on their bicycles, taking it all in. "Beware girls if your boobs are showing - the boys will be obnoxious." The beach is the main attraction for everyone. You cross over the sand dunes on a wooden walkway with hand rails on each side. Sea grape and other coastal vegetation is planted to capture the sand pebbles flying through the air before they get to the street, creating the sand dunes.

In the morning, just as the sun comes up, you see beachcombers out searching for the whelk shells, sazon cones, Junonia spotted shells, and Florida Auger, a long white pointed shell. These shells are highly desired, and look wonderful on their cocktail tables, along with the many white sand dollars found on the shore from previous forays.

Chapter 9
Cyclist

"Here they come! Here they come! Get ready!", shouts Zack at them from behind the roundabout with the metal sculpture. They wore their baseball caps backwards and had on sunglasses, being ready with one foot on the pedal, ready to bear down and dash out behind the cyclists coming down Beach Street to make the turn south onto Ocean Boulevard. The Boulevard is a double lane road with a planted middle divider of royal palms, acacia trees, and pink crape myrtles. Every weekend, cyclists, about a dozen strong, would barrel past them at 15 miles per hour, dressed in their Giro bike helmets in different colors, and long tee shirts to cover their backside while riding, designating the clubs they were members of. Cyclists shave their legs so as not to impede their speed. Hair hurts when pulled. With no hair on legs, it was good for massaging when they got cramps, and oiling them helps with the removal of dirt and grime.

The boys fall in behind the cyclists with their leader Zack, the stronger one, pedaling their asses off for about 2 miles. They pass by Sean's and Adam's neighborhood of older homes, then Zack's mobile home park. Then they pass older buildings with sea murals painted on their walls, and fly by the new condos with their bright colors of raspberry, blue, yellow, and green with white trim. The firehouse is bright red - you can't miss it. Next are the taller condos with peach walls and barrel tile roofs with parking underneath. Condo owners can just cross the Boulevard and be on the beach in minutes. The cyclists get their speed up to 30 miles per hour, and leave the boys in their dust. To the cyclists, it's all about endurance and strength.

Zack calls it quits after a two mile run. They're exhausted and their legs are tired. When they get off the bikes and are standing there, Adam says, "There's a new ice cream shop just down a bit further, called 'Cherry Tree'. Do you want to go and check it out?" They walk the bikes on the side of the road, until reaching the little shopping center. "Cherry Tree" is on the end. It sells ice cream cones, sandwiches and chips, and the "Big Gulp". Of course, they have the "Big Gulp" after that long bike ride, and sit down at one of the metal tables to sip the sodas. It's really a big soda with a long straw.

A few tables in front of them, is a mother trying to feed her Down's syndrome daughter an ice-cream cone. She has little pigtails with pink ribbons on each side of her head. She's kind of cute in her own way. The little girl is reaching out with her little chubby hands saying, "I cream, I cream". Finally, the mother gives her the cone. The little girl is trying very hard to get it to her mouth. She's not coordinated, and with a final thrust, she lands the cone right in the middle of her forehead. The ice cream is melting and running down the side of her nose. She's looking up cross eyed like a unicorn. The boys couldn't help themselves, and burst out laughing. It was so embarrassing for everyone. The mother gave them a dirty look as she was trying to clean up her little daughter. Sean was trying real hard not to laugh anymore. He got up and threw his soda in the metal trash container, and walked his bike across the street. The guys followed.

They followed a dirt path to the water, with mangroves on each side, where a small raccoon, standing on a stilt like root, was washing a crustacean with his paws. He truly looked like a little bandit with his dark markings around his eyes.

Sean took his sneakers off at the water, and waded in. As Adam and Zack did the same, Sean said "I feel bad for that mother with her daughter", crossing his eyes and waving his hands about, trying to be funny.

Adam, the more sensitive of the three, said, "Sean, you're really sick. It's tough enough having a child like that, without making fun of it. I laughed too, but it's not right."

"You're right Adam. That was insensitive of me. God forbid, I should have a poor child like that."

Suddenly, Zack says, "Guys, I have something do." He crosses back over the street and goes over to the woman and says "Madame, I'm sorry me and my buddies laughed at your daughter. That wasn't very Christian of me. I'm so sorry."

She said "Young man, I'm glad you came back. I wanted a girl and God gave me her. She will never grow up, but will be my baby always. People think she's retarded. Maybe so, but she's sweet and loving to me and I'm happy to have her. So thank you for your apology."

"Yes Madame, thank you." Zack rides his bike back to us. He says "I feel great I did the right thing."

Adam says "Zack I wish I was stronger in my religious faith, as you are. Yes, life is great if we make it that way."

Sean looks up into the clear sky and sees a flock of seagulls flying by. A white egret with its long "S" shaped neck and plumes, is standing patiently on the water's edge, waiting to stab its next meal. A group of white ibis with their curved orange beaks, are poking in the sand, and a little flurry of sand pipers comes scurrying by, poking their little beaks in the sand too, for their crustaceans. "Yup, everything is great", he says, noticing overhead a pair of grey cranes flying by with their red and black beaks.

Chapter 10

Love Bugs

It's the middle of another hot summer season in Florida. The love bugs are out in full force. These black bugs are a menace to all travelers driving on the Interstate highway system. The female bug is the bigger of the two, with the male bug attached to her rear end. She drains him dry to fertilize her eggs. Then she discards him - dead. The birds won't eat them because of their acidic bodies. These bugs smash into the cars, clouding up the windshields. Some drivers make the fatal mistake of turning their wipers on, smearing them all over the glass. Now they can't see. They have to exit the highway to find a gas station to wash them off. Zack, Adam and Sean are waiting for them, with buckets, detergent and rags, ready to go to work. After the windshields are cleaned, they use cooking spray to keep the bugs from sticking later. They pay the gas station owner ten dollars a day for use of his hose and water. He's only too glad to have the boys there. It means his business will sell more gas and food from his store.

"Charge each driver five dollars to clean the bugs off. Keep it cheap so they will hire us" Zack says.

Having fun is part of it too, spraying each other with the

hose. Adam found a new use for the bubbles, by placing them all around his chin. He looked like Abe Lincoln with blonde hair. If there was a pretty girl in the car, Zack went through great lengths to get their attention. He would lay half-way on the hood, picking at a dried love bug with his fingernail, looking through the windshield mouthing, "I love you." Some girls found this amusing. Others left their cars in disgust and went into the station's store for a soda.

One time, Sean sneaked the hose up Zack's shorts, and squirted his butt as he was flirting with some girl in the car. He jumped up in shock, and danced all over the place. The girl in the car found this to be hilarious. Zack did get her cell phone number. At the end of the day, Zack would say "How was that guys? Wasn't it worth it? We're making enough money to get us through the summer months. Let's do it again tomorrow."

Adam and Sean moan and groan, but were back the next day to reap the rewards. They may have gotten wet and tired, but each had made a small fortune. Grandpa always is saying "You want money, go work for it." It was all worth it, because none of them gets an allowance. They all worked hard that summer washing bugs off windshields.

Sean noticed his saving account approaching the three digit mark, asking Adam if his savings was doing the same.

"Yes, I'm not sure yet what I need it for, but down the road something important will come up."

"Hey Zack, are you saving your earnings?", Sean yells over to him.

"Not really, I try to put some in the bank, but end up spending it on the girls, or my father is always asking for money. I know he will never pay it back. It's a dream I guess, that he might pay it back someday. Sometimes, my mom runs out of money to pay the electric bill or such. So she asks how much do you have? Of course, I give it to her. Like my dad, she still drinks a bit too. I noticed she gets argumentative when she drinks too much. I hate arguing with her, so I call up a girl and talk."

"Like that last girl at the gas station? Are you going to talk to her?" Sean asks.

"I guess I talk to a lot of girls. I'm not getting sex or anything. I'm still trying to keep true with my bible studies. Their attention, I guess, I need. I don't get any from my father, and lately not much from my mom. She gets so controlling at times, that I have to get away from her by saying I'm going on a date. Her controlling leaves me feeling uncertain and drained. I'm losing my sense of value. So my saving account is dwindling as I spend it on girls for some sort of comfort."

Adam just listens - he's not one to ask questions.

Sean's the mouthy one. "I figure, if you don't ask, how are you going to know anything? Gee Zack, I'm sorry to hear that. We did make a lot of money this summer and you won't have much to show for it."

"Yah, I know, I just want to be happy. When we hurt others with abusive words, it's hard to find forgiveness. Such relationships cannot be healthy or life-giving", he says. "If spending my money keeps me happy, so be it."

Chapter 11

Bottle

E very Saturday and Sunday afternoon, the "Beach Bottle" has a band playing. The place is an old, one story motel on the beach, converted to a bar and hangout for the twenty one and older crowd. The new owners remodeled the ocean side wall of the motel, and installed a bamboo bar right on the beach. Telephone pole stations with thatch roofs were embedded in the sand, with waist high round shelves to put your drinks and elbows on - no chairs or stools. Colored lights were across the top of the bar, and outlined the band stage. At night, the place glowed gloriously like a Caribbean resort.

When Zack, Adam and Sean were bored, they'd bicycle the half mile down Ocean Boulevard to take in the sights, sitting on the sand in the dark shadows of the mangroves, listening to the music and watching the frolicking.

The young tourists would crowd into the place, drink beer, dance and flirt with each other. The girls wore bathing outfits with bright flowered cloths wrapped around their waist. The guys had on tank tops and swim shorts. Some had small tattoos on their upper arms. Everyone was heavily tanned.

You just couldn't return to the North without a tan, or no one would believe you were in Florida on vacation. The music was lively, with a different band playing every weekend. It was fun to be on the beach. Some girls who drank too much would take their tops off and head for the ocean, with some guy in hot pursuit. Zack particularly would take interest in this, but the owners wouldn't allow him on the property. He couldn't even buy a soda. "Under age", they said.

There wasn't much parking out front, so most tourists rode their bicycles to the place. When asked where they were going, "The Bottle", was the reply.

Down past the mangroves was another place called "Tony and His Natives". It was a pizza joint in an old beat up shack. It looked like it had been here for ages, from a more prosperous era. Inside, the walls had painted murals of scenes of Italy. The smell of garlic and rich sauces hits you hard. It hung like smoke over the dining room, and made you ready to eat.

The pizza ovens were heated up behind the counter, and waitresses were scurrying around, taking orders at the tables, and serving large platters of food.

Tony only sold one size pizza, an 18 inch. On the menu were bay scallops, pasta, grouper and rosetta du jour for the more genteel diner.

Tony's accent was thick, but his words were clear. He more than likely would give you a big hug and peck you on the cheek. Be prepared to step back if the kissing continued. It's hard for Americans to accept this greeting, but Tony means well, being from the old country.

He has dark wavy hair, is about 5 feet 10 inches tall, and is thick and fit. His English is okay, but when excited, he switches to Italian quickly.

The waitresses would be serving baskets of bread, olive oil

and vinegar for the salads. Another one would quickly uncork the bottle of wine, and fill the glasses.

It was a fun place to be, and known for Tony to break out in some Italian song, every now and then. In the corner of the restaurant, was an older man dressed in the old country styled clothes, and small straw hat, playing a mandolin. "I swear it could have been his grandfather," Sean thought.

The place was noisy, exciting, and the smells, "mama mia", so good. All the staff wore the big white aprons. Tony wore the big white Chef's hat, and wore a big fake mustache that he would wiggle for the kids, to make them laugh.

"Oops!" he is singing again. "O Sole Mio, may a pizza pie hit you in the eye," had everyone clapping and yelling "bravo!" You knew everyone was having a good time - great place to bring your family. As Tony would say, "It's the best-a-food in Flow-ree-da"

It's getting late, and it's a long bike ride home. They finished the pizza and sodas and dashed back home to Pepper Beach in the dark, not wanting their families to worry that they were out too late.

Chapter 12

School

It's lunch time in school. Sean usually hangs out with the guys in the hallway, outside of the cafeteria. Along comes Lance and his tennis team, wearing their tennis outfits with the school colors blue and white, and school letters "P.B". on the shirts. They were loud and noisy so everyone would notice them. To Sean, they looked like a pack of wolves yapping and howling around their alpha player, Lance. They took no notice of him. "Thank God", he says to himself. "Why do I feel so intimidated with them around? To think I only have to put up with them for the remainder of this year, then they will graduate and be gone."

He says to the guys, "Let's go outside. This place stinks."

Pepper Beach High School is a new school - about ten years old. It's a modern design of two story cubes, different heights, with each cube having its own blue metal roof. The walls are beige and brown brick. A walkway of white metal covers the sidewalk out front where the buses deliver the students. At the front door there's a glass window which goes straight up to the roof, and you can see right through the building.

Out front are three flagpoles - one for the American flag,

one for the State of Florida, and the low one for the high school blue flag.

An extra lane for parents dropping off their students, skirts the edge of the property, to around back, forming a loop. This is done so as not to interfere with the bus route.

From the air, the school is shaped like a "H", with the classrooms in the front, auditorium in middle, and gym and cafeteria in back.

Out back is a blue roofed-over slab of cement for outdoor dining, with blue metal picnic tables, and benches. To the left, are basketball courts and tennis courts behind a high fence and hedge. Bleachers are provided on each side of the courts.

To the right, is a big power plant with a smoke stack and an oval track field. Students from up north say the size of the school property reminds them of being on a college campus. A grassy berm goes along the back of the high school property.

Sean starts to lift weights and rope climb in gym class. He needs to be stronger and add some muscle - not like Zack who could do the rope climb hand over hand - his specialty. He could never compete with him. Zack was too strong.

In the locker room after gym exercises, the guys in his class were getting ready to take their showers. Sean noticed Zack wasn't really making an effort to change out of his gym clothes. He kept pretending that his locker needed to be tidy.

"C'mon Zack, are you going to hit the showers?" Sean asks.

"Yah, I have to. The coach has been up in arms about this. He doesn't want me to keep going to class sweaty. He knows I have been avoiding this. Deodorant doesn't help anymore. The girls say I stink after gym."

One of the guys yells out "He's afraid of being naked in front of us."

"Shut up", says Zack. "I just don't want anyone to see my junk."

Everyone dies laughing.

As usual, Zack gets embarrassed, and turns to the guys and says, "Hey, I'm not used to being naked, and I don't want to be the butt of jokes in school. If I'm being made fun of, I might have to kick some ass."

"Zack, Zack, we're all in this together. Showers are the great equalizer. Small guys show well, and big guys get intimidated. Most of us are really average."

"C'mon Zack, let's hit the showers", Sean says.

Later, walking down the hallway, Adam asks him "Did you check him out?"

"Yes, some schlong! No wonder he was concerned. He's sensitive about it. Don't talk about this. If he finds out, he'll equalize us with his fist."

"You bet. Mum's the word", says Adam with a snicker. "If only I could be so lucky."

Chapter 13

Seawall

Adam and Sean head down to the seawall facing the marina. Zack was already there. They could see his bike, a Magna, grey and black Exciter with knobby tires, lying on the grass. He was with a group of guys they knew from school.

The marina was small with its usual complements of small boats, yachts, and sailing craft, and the latest boat models available. You can hear the gonging of the halyards slapping the aluminum masts, making a hollow sound. Nearer to them were two large ships. One with a blue hull with "N.O.V.A." on the side, and another white ship with "The Explorer, Wood's Hole", lettered on the hull. These vessels did a lot of exploration off the coast, especially along the reefs.

Across the marina were two small white fuel storage tanks, a crane, and ice house. Many a fisherman would sell their day's catch to the local restaurants and other business men standing at these docks. It smelled fishy in this area, so the boys didn't venture on their bikes down there too often. The sports fishermen stood under a big sign, which said, "Pepper Beach, Florida, Home of the Groupers", and took pictures and congratulated each other.

As the small craft and yachts were sailing out the inlet to the ocean, Zack and the rest of the group would wave at people they knew, and cat call to the girls in their bikinis, sunbathing on the top decks of the boats.

Behind them was the rejuvenated park. A few years back, there was a drive to raise money by selling paver patio squares, to develop this land on the edge of the inlet to the beach.

The walkways wound in and around clumps of royal palms, and grassy shrubbery, with benches facing the water. The elderly people loved walking along here holding hands or doing their Chinese exercises. The tourists would walk along the pavers with their heads down, reading the inscriptions on them. Some found great amusement with what some people had stamped on them: "My best friend, Bullet", Sean guessed that guy had a dog. "Love you always, Susie". Another one, is a funny one - "From your dead beat husband". The next paver must have been from his mad wife. It said "Drop Dead." There was always laughter coming from the new arrivals as they read these pavers.

One of the guys asks, "Zack you're always hanging around the girls. Are you getting any action?"

Zack takes his hat off and scratches his head. "Well, I almost did once."

"How close did you get?" Adam asks.

"Well, I met this girl, Tess, on the beach one afternoon. I sat with her most of the day. We talked and rubbed sun tan lotion on each other. It was getting dark. She suggested we sit up at the pavilion, on the table. Next thing you know I had my hand under her halter top. She finally took it off."

"Hang those beach towels up on the hanger poles", she said, "so people can't see us from the street."

"We started making out, and I was on top of her, when her crazy fat mother comes bursting through the towels swinging her big purse, screaming, 'You pervert! You pervert!' I fell off the table, grabbed my swim shorts and ran like hell into the night. I came back later and got my beach towel and wrote in the sand, "I love you Tess".

All the guys burst out laughing and started slapping each other on their backs until one of them almost fell in the water. They had to grab him quickly from the seawall.

"Ya know guys, I'm going to stay a virgin - it's too dangerous out there. It's best I read the Bible to stay clean and true." said Zack.

The guys laughed some more, others fell on the grass and rolled around. Zack said, "Screw you", and got on his bike to ride home.

"If I stay any longer" he yells back, "I'm going to have beat the crap out of you". Zack doesn't like to be embarrassed. Sean thought it was a bit unfair when that fat mother called Zack a rotten name. Many parents have no idea what their teenage children are doing. "They just don't do those things", are their comments. There's always a gap between what parents perceive, and reality. Children are selfish and inconsiderate.

Lots of twelve, thirteen and fourteen year olds are participating in "Yum". That's where girls do favors to boys for money, for popularity or dates. Sometimes, the boys demand this of their girlfriends. "It's not sex", they say, because there's no penetration, so they won't get a STD or baby, "if it feels good, do it". "They forgot, it is a penetration, just below their brains - called a mouth", Sean says to himself.

Zack said he never took part in any of this stuff. He was chaste until he tried something with a girl he liked, only to be scared away by a purse swinging mama. Sean was sure Zack would remain chaste for the rest of his high school years - "not like him, a virgin who still wants to find out what all the fuss is about", he thought.

Chapter 14

Dentist

Adam quit playing varsity basketball in his junior year, once he bought his first horse, an appaloosa, with the money he had earned that summer washing cars. He spent all his time, after high school, at the stables, where he boarded his horse. He chose the appaloosa because of its white and brown markings on the rump, knowing the Great Plain Indians favored this breed. They were considered a great warrior with a painted face, on a painted horse, getting ready to go into battle. It has something to do with the Great Spirit. Adam thought his horse was the most beautiful of all the breeds of horses. He'd spend hours grooming and brushing his tail and mane. Making a deal with his dentist, David, to keep his stables clean and care for his four horses, meant free board. Often, he would come home sweaty and tired. His mother worried, but he assured her that all was well with the work and the horse.

Many times, Adam was asked by David to accompany him and his family on weekend rides through the forest along the back of his property. His children would wear their colorful helmets, as well as his wife. David wore a cowboy hat. Adam wore his baseball cap and sunglasses.

They would slowly ride for hours through the palmetto palms and saw grasses. Sometimes they would spot a deer, an owl or fox. Very rarely did they encounter a black bear. If the horses scented a bear around, you had to keep a tight rein on them, or they would bolt.

As Adam became more attached to the dentist's family, he was staying over for dinner and playing more with the two children. After dinner, games and cards were placed on the dining room table. David's wife introduced the game "ball and jacks". David's wife, a former high school beauty queen, was from a small western Texas town. She met him while attending a nearby College of Dentistry. They fell in love and married shortly thereafter and upon David's graduation, moved to Florida, to start his practice in his home town of Pepper Beach, where his father had given him 50 acres with an old stable on it. Everyone tried to become skillful, tossing the small ball in the air and scooping up as many jacks as you could. With the darkness of winter coming earlier, these games entertained the family immensely. Later, the wife would serve hot chocolate and popcorn, while everyone was watching television or playing videos.

David admired Adam and his ability to relate to his children. Adam knew how to talk to them and explain things. When sitting on the couch, the children would press up against him and even fall asleep with his arms around them. He was a great playmate, like a big brother.

Adam sometimes slept in the stables when he stayed too late. There was an old stable hands apartment at the end of the stalls, with a bed, a chest of drawers, and small bath with a shower. David's wife would give him sheets and towels to stay out there. Adam would call his parents on his cell phone to say he was staying overnight, then catch the school bus, out front, the next morning to get to school.

Adam would volunteer to watch the children every time David and his wife had to go out of town. He was at their every "beck and call", and felt part of their family.

Adam's home life was a quiet setting. His father, a thin fragile man who wore eyeglasses, worked for the water company, and read a lot. His mother, also thin, with hair starting to turn gray on the edges, in her late fifties, was overly religious. She read her bible and visited with her sister in town. His own family was not socially active. They didn't socialize much or take long vacations for that matter. It was uneventful, with nothing exciting happening.

Adam's home life was boring and he felt lonely at times. David's family offered the activities that normal families do. Adam craved it. Being an adopted child, he would never know much about his real parents. All he knew was that they lived poorly and had him as unmarried teenagers. It was better for him to be put up for adoption and have a better life, which he did get. David found Adam's adoption story interesting, and wanted to know more by asking questions that Adam didn't have the answers available to him at that time.

Chapter 15

Adoption

She sat there quietly, smoking her cigarette, watching her baby boy. He was almost one year old, playing on the floor with a little toy, a quiet boy who never really fussed or cried except when he was hungry or uncomfortable. She took another puff of her cigarette, as he looked up at her with his blue eyes, blonde hair and a sweet smile. She just watched.

Her boyfriend - they were not married yet - would be home later. They lived in an old trailer on the edge of an open area with woods all around them. It was sort of a lonely place. He worked hard in the iron mines up here in Northern Michigan. Both their families were from this area. They had their baby out of wedlock and it was hard keeping up with daily needs.

Her boyfriend was not educated enough, and she barely passed high school herself. She thought, "This is no life for her child - a life of poverty and drudgery." There were times when there wasn't enough food to eat. Her boyfriend, who promised to marry her one day, was drinking his paycheck up in the local pool hall with his buddies. He'd come home a bit under the weather, and crash on the couch. She felt he wasn't really ready for marriage or a family. They were still teenagers, and life was hard.

She planted a small garden out back; raising corn, peas, string beans, squash, some potatoes and tomatoes. It wouldn't be enough to live on, but at least she was trying to have some food in the home.

Her son looked like his father, with blonde hair and blue eyes. His disposition was like hers - quiet, trusting and smart.

She named her son Adam. Coming from a family of all unmarried sisters, this would be his name for being the first male born into her family. She loved the way he smelled and how bubbles would form at his lips when he got excited.

After she gave birth to Adam, she checked all his fingers and toes to see if he was perfect. A nurse came into her hospital room with some papers and a pen.

"Sign this." the nurse says.

"What is it?" she asks.

"It's an authorization to give him a circumcision."

"What's that?" she asks, not knowing what this meant.

The nurse explains why it was necessary to perform the circumcision for boys. "He will feel no pain. He will be alright, I assure you."

"Where is my man when I need him the most?" she says. She reluctantly signed the paper, rolled over on her side and cried "They're going to hurt my baby." She was from an all girl family and didn't know of these things. It was never discussed. She felt so ignorant.

She and her boyfriend discussed adoption for Adam. They realized they weren't prepared to take care of a baby. Arrangements had been made with Catholic Social Services to have Adam adopted by a couple from Florida.

The nuns try to teach these young, unwed mothers, how

to raise their babies to be healthy and how to prevent having more babies, by use of condoms. It breaks your heart when they get no postnatal instructions from home. They don't know what foods babies eat or how to change a diaper. They know nothing of most common ailments of newborns.

Somehow these young teenaged mothers think having a baby will make everything wonderful, but the challenges overwhelm them and most will give up their babies. The nuns are waiting to assist.

It's time, she thought, to bring him to town. The boyfriend left her his old white pickup truck for the eight mile ride. His work buddies picked him up for work that day.

She parked outside the mustard yellow wooden building with dark green trim. There was a thin black cross and sign Catholic Social Services, St. Vincent attached to the outside wall. She brought Adam in with a tote bag filled with his stuff, like diapers, bottles, blanket, his favorite toys and whatever else she could find.

The nun greeted her and asked if she was ready to surrender Adam. Everything had been prearranged, and documents signed, a few days before. In a whisper, she said, "yes." The nun took the baby from her arms, and disappeared through a door. She knew that a young barren couple from Florida wanted a boy. They came this far north to adopt him, on one condition from the baby's mother - that his name was to remain Adam. They agreed.

She went over to the door and listened, then she opened it a crack to see Adam being put in the arms of his new adoptive mother. She was a small lean woman in her young thirties wearing a long floral dress down to her knees. She knew it was for the best. Adam would have a good life. Then she quietly closed the door, sat down in a chair in this cold, unfurnished room, covering her eyes with her hands, and wept deeply for the loss of her baby.

Chapter 16

Stables

t was getting late and David was ready to go to bed. He adjusted his eyeglasses as he looked out the window one last time. The stable lights were still on. There were no shadows moving about the entrance. "Did Adam forget to turn the lights off before he went home?", he says to himself.

He went out to check to see if everything was alright. The stables were down in the corner of the property, backed up to the forest. Fencing was around the stables to keep the horses from wandering too far from the barn. It was made of old vertical boards, never painted - just brown and black from age. A low gable roof was of old metal panels. Big sliding doors on old tracks were on each end, but never closed.

It was quiet. The horses were cared for with hay spread down in the stalls. They were eating their oats. The rake was against the wall and Adam's shirt was hanging on a peg. David walked down to the other end of the barn. There were eight stalls. The horses were in five of them, with the remaining stalls containing the bales of hay and large bags of oats. The last area had a tack room and small horse handler's apartment.

He heard a noise of shuffling of hay in the last empty stall. He looked through the bars at the top of the gate. There was Adam with his back to him. His shirt was off and his jeans down at his feet. David marveled at Adam's lean back, shaped like a "V", and how his muscles were moving slowly beneath the skin. "What a beautiful sight he was", David thought. He remained still, watching Adam, until there was a moan, then stillness. Slowly, David backed away and quietly left the area for the evening.

The next night, after dinner, Adam was back in the stables putting fresh hay down. It was hot, so he had his shirt off as he always does. Quietly, he was humming to himself, going about his business, and when he turned around he got a "start" with David standing there, watching him. David was six feet tall, medium brown hair, short cut, with intense blue eyes behind his stylish eyeglasses. He dressed conservatively with loafers, khaki pants and a light colored long sleeve shirt with cuffs rolled up.

"Hi David", Adam said. "I'm working a bit late tonight, because I had to play basketball."

"That's okay, Adam. You shouldn't have to work so hard", David said.

"I know, I just want to do my part for the free boarding of my horse", said Adam.

"I saw the lights on late last night, so I came over to check. I thought you forgot to turn them off."

"No, I was busy."

"I know, I watched you in the empty stall." said David.

"Oh I'm so embarrassed. I didn't mean for that to happen", Adam says.

"Don't worry Adam. We all have had our moments. When I was your age, I did the same thing too. You know you're a beautiful young man. How about next time I help you?"

Adam was shocked to hear this coming from David. All he could do was look at him with a blank face, stunned, with his mouth open.

Chapter 17

Hurt

Sean met Zack at the ice cream stand down near the beach. He was getting a milk shake. Sean decided to get one too.

"Sean, did you hear what happened to Adam last night?" Zack asked.

"No, I didn't. What happened?"

"They took Adam away to a 'funny farm'."

"Why?"

"I heard he burned the dentist's stables down. They found him just beyond the light of the fire, babbling about something. He went crazy and started screaming. The medical people had to strap him down on the gurney and medicate him."

"Oh my gosh! Will he be okay?"

"Nobody knows", Zack said.

The evening before, when Adam was cleaning out the stalls and brushing the horses down, David showed up in the barn to tell him that his family and he were leaving Florida to go out West to start a new practice. His wife wanted to be closer to her family.

Adam was stunned. "What about me? Can you take me with you?"

"No I can't", David said. "Everything is settled."

"But…..but, you said you loved me and wanted to be near me", Adam said.

"No, I said I cared for you."

"Can we write or call each other?" Adam asks.

"No, I don't think that would be a good idea. I have to think about my family first."

"Am I going to get the five acres you promised me for working so hard in the stables?"

"No, the sale is done and the plot remains unchanged. I don't believe I said that to you. I wouldn't want to explain that to my wife."

"Yes, you did. Why do you think I worked so hard for you, grooming all your horses and babysitting your children when you had to go out of town. I did this because I thought we loved one another - that someday this would all be worth it" Adam exclaimed.

"Well, the time has come for you to get on with your life, Adam."

"My life!", Adam screamed. "My life! It was all for us! I believed in you and now you are leaving and throwing me aside. What kind of freak have you become?"

With this outburst from Adam, David turns his back on him and heads back to his house, leaving Adam standing there with his fists clenched at his sides. Tears were streaming down his face, his eyes glazed over.

"How could he hurt me so bad? I gave him my heart. I would have done anything he asked of me. And now….he just turns and walks away. You will pay, you rotten bastard, you ass wipe! I hope you die", he screams. "You will pay", as rage comes over him.

Adam turns and goes back into the stables. He lets loose David's four horses into the pasture nearby.

Then he grabs a pitchfork, and piles high the dry hay into every corner of the barn and stalls. He latches shut the door to the stall where his horse is, and goes to the little apartment in back to retrieve matches next to the candle on the chest of drawers - the candle they lit when staying together. Then he lights the hay on fire, in the four corners of the barn.

He goes out the back door and stands in the dark shadows crying. Soon his horse is whinnying in fear, and starts to kick the side boards of the barn to escape. With each kick, Adam screams. He knows the fire will consume his horse, the only thing that was totally his, the one thing he loved the most.

The barn is becoming an inferno. The horse is screaming with fear and pain. Adam is in a complete state of emotional anguish, tearing at his hair and then tearing at his skin on his chest, leaving rivulets of blood with his fingernails. He wanted to run into the flaming barn and lay on his horse and die too, but the intensity of the fire propels him back.

As the roof caves in, the whinnying stops. The fire storm makes a huge noise, sucking the air in to fuel its fury.

Adam falls to the ground with deep sobs, pounding the earth with his fists, falling into the deepest pain imaginable, until his head touches the ground. Through this pain will come his purification. A fireman discovers him this way, whimpering, and calls the ambulance attendants to take care of him.

Chapter 18

Fire

They had just finished dinner, when David noticed a flickering glow coming through the French doors in the dining room. He got up from the table to look outside. Then he yells to his wife, "Call the fire department!"

"What's wrong?" she asks.

"The stables are on fire and the horses are loose and galloping all over the front pasture trying to avoid the flames." he said.

David runs out to the pasture and opens a side gate to let the horses escape into another area for safe keeping. He thought he heard some wailing, but couldn't pinpoint the direction it was coming from. It was too dark. The stables now were an inferno with sparks flying up into the air.

"Where was Adam's horse?" he said to himself. "I didn't see it running with the other horses into the side pasture."

He could hear a horse whinnying in the inferno, and some more wailing coming from the back of the stables near the woods.

The fire trucks had arrived with an ambulance, which always accompanies them in case anyone gets hurt.

The firemen were dragging their hoses to the back of the stable area to douse any sparks. They didn't want the forest to catch on fire.

One fireman noticed Adam kneeling in the grass at the end of the pasture. He had his shirt off and looked like he had been burned. The fireman went to see how he was doing.

He said Adam was babbling something. It sounded like, "That rotten bastard." Adam's eyes were glazed over. One fireman said, "You could see the flames in his eyes."

Later, another fireman yells "Hey Chief, looks like a fried horse in the last stall! Has white and brown markings on its rump." Someone said, "It's Adam's horse, the appaloosa."

"Why would he not try to get his horse out of the stables?" a fireman asks. "Why didn't he save it?"

Only Adam knew the answer to that question. He was totally defeated. He felt betrayed by the dentist and wanted to destroy any reminders of him, including his horse, which he loved so dearly.

The medical people tried to help Adam, but he started screaming. They strapped him to a gurney and medicated him. David and his family were standing off to the side as they wheeled Adam past. His face was towards them, with hate in his eyes.

"What's happening Mommy?", the little girl asks.

"I don't know, I'm not sure what's happening", she said, as she looked at her husband.

David knew. He knew what he had done to that boy - what he said, what he promised. But he kept quiet, not saying a word, just to save his skin, as tears flowed down his cheeks from under his eyeglasses. He just stood there with his arm around his son, as the ambulance pulled away.

Chapter 19

Junior Year

Sean was 17 years old and entering his junior year in high school. He was beginning to feel lonely without Adam around. Zack had another girlfriend, so he didn't see him much lately either.

During lunch period, Sean noticed a bunch of guys heading for the tennis courts. They were gone the whole lunch period. Sean wondered what they were doing. This was a daily occurrence. The next day, he followed them into the tennis courts and walked behind the bleachers with them. Some of the senior boys were already there smoking. He knew it was marijuana by its pungent smell. One of the seniors came over and passed him his joint.

"Want a hit?", he asks.

"No, I don't smoke", Sean says.

"Hey, it won't hurt you. You might like it. Here, try it."

Sean takes the rolled joint and has a puff. Wow! He started to cough and gag. His eyes started to tear. Handing him back the joint, he said, "Who could ever smoke this stuff? It tastes like crap."

"You got to take a few more hits before you get used to it", the senior says.

The joint is being passed around to all the guys, some even younger than Sean. The word "pot head" comes to mind. It seemed to him they were all talking weird - words like "cool, hey man, how's your mama". Trying another puff seems to go down easier. By now, everyone was laughing and not making any sense.

A strange feeling came across Sean, like euphoria. Everything being said was very clear, even though it wasn't. Colors were brighter, sounds lucid. He didn't have a care in the world. What a sensation! What a perception! This smoking unlocks something in the brain to make like he's listening to himself - feeling like nothing mattered.....he was rubber. They headed back to their classes when the school bell rang. Lunch period is over. The rest of the day felt weird sitting in his classes with a smirk on his face like knowing something and not telling. The feeling was good, but he couldn't focus on his studies for the rest of the day.

The school buses were in front of the school waiting to take the students home. Sean was very hungry from not eating lunch. When he got home he headed straight to the kitchen, opening the refrigerator to grab what's available, and stuffed his face.

"My, my, aren't you the hungry one. Didn't you eat lunch today?", asks grandma.

"No, grandma, I got stuck at the tennis court with the guys and didn't have time to eat."

"Okay young man, slow down. We'll be eating dinner soon. Go to your room and freshen up", she says.

At dinner, he ate two helpings of spaghetti and meatballs, a salad and drink, then helped grandma clean the kitchen.

Excusing himself to his bedroom, he laid on the bed and enjoyed the pensiveness.

The next day at lunch time, he couldn't wait to get back to the tennis courts. The same group was there puffing away. A joint was shared and being passed around. One of the seniors asked him if he would like to buy a bag of weed and papers to roll and make his own joints.

"How much?", Sean asked.

"Ten dollars."

Sounded cheap enough to him, so he paid for the bag and returned to class.

During that week, Sean rolled his joints and puffed away. He was hooked.

Going back, a week later, to buy his second bag of weed, the price shot up to forty dollars a bag.

"Why the higher price?"

"Supply and demand", the senior says. "The first bag was a 'come on'. This is the normal price of weed - forty bucks for a two gram bag."

Sean needed it and paid for it. He liked how it made him feel. It got so that he didn't care if he learned anything in class. The teachers were jerks and classes are boring. He was becoming a malingerer, by not going to classes. Instead, he walked around the school buildings. At home, he watched television too much and didn't do his chores. He gave up playing sports and quit the basketball team, hating the practice, doing it over and over again - so boring.

He wouldn't turn in his homework, keeping it in his backpack on the floor, and please, don't assign him any projects - he hates doing them.

Sean starts failing in school, and didn't want to talk to anyone, having nothing to say. Everyone is fake, even the cops are fakes and dirty. He wouldn't go to the gym or take showers, always feeling tired and lethargic.

Grandpa started to yell at him in the mornings to get up and catch the school bus. He was not enthusiastic about driving Sean to school because he was sleeping in later.

"Sean, pick up your clothes, your bedroom stinks. We didn't raise you to be like this."

With grandpa getting angry all the time, Sean stopped smoking inside his bedroom and kept the window open to blow the smoke outside so the bedroom wouldn't smell like a dirty ashtray.

Grandpa still kept on yelling, "Sean, strip your bed! If you don't want to wash your clothes, at least get them to the laundry room, and I'll wash them for you."

The school counselor called to tell grandpa and grandma that Sean wasn't attending all the classes and that his grades were suffering. If he didn't improve, they might have to hold him back a year, suggesting a therapist.

Sean's grandparents were very concerned. They sat him down at the kitchen table to explain how they live on social security and didn't have much money to pay for these treatments.

Sean spent some time going to a few sessions with the therapist, who explained how smoking weed would make the mind cloudy and cause the loss of motivation. He would become an underachiever and lazy. He knew that was true. He also noticed a loss of friends. By not calling them, they stopped calling him. Sean was becoming unhappy. The therapist pointed this out. In his mind, these sessions were a waste of his grandparents' money, so he stopped going.

Sean's grandparents were beside themselves. They knew he smoked weed and didn't know what to do. Finally, grandpa said, "If he wants to fail, let him. Let him fall in a ditch and decide if he wants to live or die." Grandma cried. She started not combing her hair and looking a bit unkempt. Every time she'd see Sean coming home, from wherever, she would shake her head and go to her room, sit in her lounge chair with Puffy on her lap and silently cry. Grandpa wouldn't talk to him. He was so angry, yet, he kept right on top of him to do the chores, clean the room, bathe and get to school on time. Sean considers him a nag.

Chapter 20

Party

Brad, a senior from high school, invited Sean to a pizza party at his home that coming weekend. His parents were out of town for a two week vacation, so the condo was all to himself.

That afternoon, Sean pedaled his bicycle down the Boulevard to the complex of second level homes with parking underneath, where Brad lived. Noticing some bicycles already there in the parking area below the home, he walked up the wooden stairs to the landing and knocked on the door. Brad opened the door, emitting a swirl of smoke. You could smell the odor of marijuana, it was so strong.

The party was already underway with bong smoking, a glass tube with a glass ball on the bottom, which looks like a vase. Five guys were already there puffing away. So was Boomer, sitting on the floor taking his turn at the bong.

"Hey Dude," he says.

Sean can see some marks around Boomer's eyes. His eyes were also bloodshot from so much smoking. He's not a particularly good looking guy. His head is shaped like a peanut shell, with a 2 inch high, sort of red, flat top. Silver rings are in his stretched ear lobes. People obsessed with this type of ear jewelry are called "gauge kings", and he also has a silver stud in his nose - something Sean would never do. He thinks Boomer has a psychiatric disorder and has harmed himself, with his addiction. Sean wonders about Boomer's "I.Q." He probably has poor memory and can't even remember Sean's name.

"What am I thinking? I don't even know his real name - no one does. Is he a senior? Does he even go to my school? I have never seen him there, but he seems to show up for all pot smoking episodes."

All the guys are from high school and Sean was one of the younger ones. He sat on the floor and got the bong passed to him. You have to suck the smoke coming from the burning weed in a chamber below, up through the water. It's something like a water filtering device. It's a bit of effort to suck it up, and it's supposed to filter out the toxic components. The THC, the main active ingredients in weed, will be more intense. It will also slow down your thinking process. The smoke is cool to his throat, and tastes like candy corn. Too much smoking will cause coughing from the deeper inhalation into their lungs. Boomer is really into the bong. His coughing is more pronounced than the rest of them. He's throwing out dark mucus.

The pizza boy arrives with boxes of pizza. He stands back on the landing, near the railing, when the door is open. The smoke and smell is overwhelming. He waves his hand across his face to keep the smoke away. Sean notices Brad gave him a nice tip. They all dive into the pizza pies. They're super hungry by now. Beer and soda cans are tossed on the floor, and scattered across the table surfaces.

The guys are starting to use the bathroom. Their peeing isn't the best. Urine is splattered on the white tiled floor. One guy is peeing in the tub. "Can't miss this one bro", he says.

Boomer is in the bathroom on the floor, admiring all the

urine pattern swirls. The guys have to go in and drag him out. He's talking not too coherently. He's wasted. "Hey bro, can't you see the clarity of the pattern? It's saying something to me. Let's get a camera and take pictures. It's art man!", says Boomer.

Now Sean knows smoking from a bong will drop you down quickly. Actually, Brad said he put "King Kong" weed into the burning chamber. It's home grown without all the fertilizers, and also has a nice burn, and a great high.

The guys were all coming down fast - euphoria sliding over all and making them fall asleep on the couch and floor. Sean remembers waking up early the next morning. The sun was coming up slowly and sending beams of sunlight across the carpeted floor. Slowly each guy would wake up.

One guy, wiping his eyes, said, "Wow, that was some trip!"

Another one said, "Hey, did you know Jefferson grew pot on his plantation during colonial America?"

"Hey guys, I got one better", another guy says. "Levi's first jeans were made from weed. I wish I had a pair on now, then I"d really be smoking."

Sean asks, "Where do you guys get this stuff?"

"I don't know. Read it somewhere", they said.

The younger guy reveals that "My grandfather is telling the spirits to come and visit him. How cool is that?"

Sean was feeling a bit sick and tired from smoking too much. It was time for him to bike home, eat a breakfast and crawl into his bed. He wanted grandma to see him home and safe. She always worries about him.

If only he didn't have to face grandpa again and hear him keep nagging on having a clean bedroom and picking up his clothes.

"What a turd", he says.

Chapter 21

Stealing

Sean was running out of his summer earnings, fast, paying forty dollars for a bag of weed. He went around the neighborhood washing cars, mowing lawns, raking leaves and picking up the dropped coconuts from the trees lining his streets. Still, it wasn't enough money for the amount of weed he was smoking weekly.

So he started using his lunch money and not eating lunch. In the next few months he lost twenty pounds in body weight, and got that hollow look in the face. Stealing clothes from the stores in the Mall to sell, was so easy. The stores didn't have a clue.

Later, he started taking grandpa's quarters in a bowl on the dresser, which wasn't enough money. Stealing ten dollars from grandma's purse every week helped. He didn't want to take too much as to make her suspicious, trying to act normal, even though he had become sneaky and untrustworthy.

A "pot head" told Sean of a party coming up in an old, abandoned house this Saturday, and did he want to go? He picked Sean up in his car down on the Boulevard and off they headed into town, but first he had to go buy some weed for himself. They drove to a biker's bar called "Cowboy Electric" off Main Street. It was a cement block building, painted dark burgundy with a lighted cowboy sign out front. The building had no windows, but Sean could hear the music every time someone opened the front door.

There was lots of noise from the cycles' mufflers, and swirls of dust from the tremendous amount of activity. The boys parked across the street in a dirt parking area waiting for the pot dealer to show up.

Finally, pot head sees dealer, a big fat muscular guy with his girlfriend riding pillion on his motor cycle. She was not pretty, being plump with her stomach exposed, striped shorts and black engineer boots, with tattoos running up and down her arms.

Sean did not feel comfortable waiting in the car, while pot head was making the deal with the biker on the side of the night club.

In looking around, Sean spots a deputy sheriff's car down a dark side street. His lights were off, while observing the crowd, coming and going.

Pot head returns to the car and says, "I got my stash. Do you want to buy some?"

"No, there's a cop car down the street. Let's get out of here before we're hauled off to jail."

They locate the abandoned house in an older neighborhood with the lawn not mowed and junk lying all around then noticed as they went into the house, an old mattress on the floor, with a naked girl and naked guy on it, passed out. Another guy was getting lizard scales drawn on his face by some girl with a black marker - both were "out of it." What a surprise lizard face would get the next day when he looked in the mirror.

A "roach" was passed to Sean so he had a puff. That got him started down the halls of melancholy. The "bong" was next.

Everyone was laughing at using words like "die-o and Ivory", which they found hilarious. Sean didn't see the humor in it. Someone brought a laptop and was showing a classmate from school on Facebook, holding a bottle of vodka, grape juice and a bag of weed. Later it was discovered that he was playing Russian roulette, all doped up, and shot himself in the head, dead. Sean brushed it off - that wasn't going to happen to him.

He didn't come home that night - too "blitzed". Grandpa and grandma stopped asking him where he was going. He knew his family was upset and didn't want this to be happening.

The therapist said that drugs mask deep seated problems, and that he was throwing his life away. Sean didn't put much thought into what the therapist was saying. He wanted what the smoking gave him - more freedom, more staying out with friends, listening to music, playing videos, and hanging out. Nothing mattered - his mind was inactive. Having no idea what to do about the future, didn't matter. He felt good and needed more weed and had no money.

The next day during gym class after everyone left the locker room to go play basketball or climb the ropes and rings, Sean went to Zack's locker. He knew the combination. No one was around, and, needing the money, Sean opens Zack's gym locker, took Zack's wallet out, and pocketed forty bucks, then put everything back into the locker. As he was doing this, a student coming around the back of the lockers, saw him in Zack's locker. He stopped, watched a few seconds, and then backed up and headed back into the gym without saying anything to anyone. He knew Sean was Zack's best friend and didn't want any trouble.

When gym class was over and the showering done, Zack went to his locker to change into his clothes, and noticed that his wallet wasn't in the right pocket. He opened his wallet and saw that forty dollars was missing.

He looked around the bench area, anger in his face, and said, "Who stole my money?" Everyone stopped dressing and said all at once "Not me, not me."

"Someone took my money." said Zack loudly. "Who took it?" He started walking down along the benches, grabbed each guy by the shirt and said "Where is it?" Everyone was scared.

They know of Zack's way of doling out punishment. Zack grabbed the last guy who was shaking badly. Zack said "You're the last one - you took my money."

"No-no, Zack, believe me I would never do anything like that to you."

"But you do know, don't you?"

"Yes, Sean took it. I saw him at the beginning of class in your locker, taking something. I swear to you."

Zack leans his head back with his fists clenched at his side and let out a scream. "Ahhhhhh."

The guys, half dressed, grabbed their clothes and cleared out of the locker room. They could hear Zack smashing at the locker doors with his fists, because of his best friend's betrayal.

In twenty minutes, it was all over the school that Sean was a thief. There was going to be hell to pay.

Sean was long gone from school by now. He bought his bag of weed from the senior behind the tennis bleachers, and headed to the back of the school property, up over the grass berm into the woods beyond. Sitting down on the ground under a big oak tree, he rolled his joint and puffed, and puffed, and puffed.

Chapter 22

Anger

When Sean got to school the next day, Friday, he was confident that Zack didn't know who stole his money. He was at his locker, on the second floor near the stairwell, when realizing that there were more students on the second floor than ever before. Getting ready to go to his homeroom, Sean saw Zack coming from the other end of the hall through the crowd. He was a head taller than most and easy to spot. The crowd opened up for him like the "parting of the Red Sea". That's when Sean knew that Zack was coming for the stolen money. The stern look on his face said it all. Sean was frozen to the spot and couldn't move, hearing the comments coming from the students. "There he is, the crook. He'd probably steal from his mother. Man, is he going to get his just do now."

Zack came up to Sean, grabbed him by the shirt, and lifted him off the floor three inches, with one arm. His toes were barely touching the floor. Lifting him so their eyes were even, he said "Where is my money?"

Sean could hardly talk with his hand against his throat,

and fear was in his eyes, knowing what Zack was capable of doing. "I....don't .....have......it", choking as he talked.

"What did you do with it?" Zack asks.

"Spent.......on weed," Sean chokingly answered.

"Weed?" he shouts. "You spent it on weed - the Devils Tool?"

With that, he punches Sean in the stomach two times with his free hand. "You scumbag, you rotten shit head!", he screams.

He lifts all 125 pounds of Sean up over his head with both hands, and heads for the stairwell twenty feet from his locker. The crowd wants to see blood and broken bones. They're yelling "Throw him down the stairs Zack, throw him down! The bastard is no good!"

Zack doesn't see gray in his anger, only black and white. His justice is firm and swift. Don't ever cross him. He's not a bully, but he will deal with the problem quickly. Even the senior boys won't mess with him, no matter how big they are.

Some girl students start to scream. They know what Zack will do and are scared for Sean. With all the screaming and noise in the hallway, some teachers came out of their classrooms to see what all the commotion was about.

Mr. Crews, his homeroom teacher, rushed out into the crowd. He's a bit taller than Zack, has dark hair and dark rimmed eyeglasses, and is wearing a pale blue dress shirt and tie. He yells in his booming voice, "Zack put him down! Put him down immediately!"

Zack turns, with Sean still over his head, looks at Mr. Crews, and drops him to the floor. "I think he bounced", someone said. Zack gives Sean two swift kicks with his boots, in the stomach, and says, "Sean, have my money here Monday morning, or else you'll really taste my leather boots."

He was curled up into a ball on the floor, holding his stomach, hurting so bad. Zack moved off down the hallway to his homeroom. The crowd breaks up. The din of noise quiets down. The crowd is disappointed. Sean had wet his pants.

Mr. Crews comes over to help him up. While sitting against the lockers, he asks, "Are you okay Sean?"

"I think so", as he feels the rib cage. "No broken ribs, just a bit sore and humiliated."

"Sean", Mr. Crews asks, "what is this all about?"

"I took some of his money."

"Oh," says Mr. Crews with his hand rubbing his chin. "Sean, you'd better clear this up. Zack won't let this go until you settle it."

"I know that for sure", struggling to get up. "Mr. Crews, I don't think I will be in homeroom this morning. I hurt a little bit." He walked over to the stairwell and looked down. It's all cement with an iron rail on the side. The stairs go down six steps, turn and go down another six steps to the first floor. A big window is there. He visualizes his frail body laying there on the landing, knowing he would have ended up in the hospital.

The first bell of the day started to ring. Everyone is seated in their homerooms. Mr. Crews leaves for his classroom, with a glance back at Sean, and shakes his head.

He left the school, going out the back door, hobbling across the oval track and up the grassy berm to the woods beyond. Finding his favorite tree, he sat down, reached into his pocket, and pulled out a joint and lights up for a puff. "Now the pain will subside a bit", he says out loud. While sitting there smoking, he starts to consider where is he going to get money to pay Zack off. Nothing comes immediately to mind.

Chapter 23

Beaten Puppy

Sean arrived home from school holding his sore stomach. The "joints" he smoked helped a little in easing the pain from Zack's punches and kicks.

Grandma asks, "Are you alright?"

"I just feel a little sick to my stomach." he says.

"Oh, Uncle Preston is coming over tonight to have dinner with us, and is staying the weekend to watch the house and Puffy", says grandma. "We're going on a short cruise out of Cape Canaveral tomorrow morning, early."

This was the first time he heard this. It wasn't like them to keep secrets from him, but who was he to talk, being always secretive this past year, with the smoking and all.

"Okay, Grandma, I'm going to lay down for a while. I'm not sure if I'll be hungry enough to have dinner with you and Preston. I don't feel well."

That night, while Uncle Preston was having dinner with his parents, Sean just stayed in his room being quiet.

At dinner, grandma tells Preston that Sean was smoking marijuana and they just didn't know what to do. He was stealing money from them. Grandpa has to hide his wallet and she has to be careful where she puts her purse. Besides, she didn't want him home alone, having one of those "druggie" parties. "They could wreck my home", she says.

The next morning, Saturday, grandma and grandpa left very early to be at the cruise ship. He didn't see them to say have a good trip, guessing they didn't expect it anyway.

Preston was having a coffee and toast in the kitchen. Sean took a bowl and had cereal.

"Want to go to the beach with me and watch volleyball?", Preston asks.

"Yuh, that will be fine." Then after eating a bowl of cereal, Sean went to his room to change, and came out with a bathing suit on. The waistband wasn't even near his waist, because of all the weight he had lost.

"Wow", says Preston. You are so skinny. Your arms and legs are like toothpicks. You look anemic. Aren't you eating?"

"No, I'm not hungry most of the time."

"You know Sean, I know about the pot smoking. Are you aware of the dangers you are forming for yourself?"

"Yes", he said. "the therapist told me all about them. I didn't want to hear any more. It was a waste of money."

Uncle Preston said, "In many ways you are still like a child. Your brains aren't fully developed and there are consequences for the things you consider cool, and they can be deadly, like all this weight you're losing. It's unhealthy. Some of your systems can shut down", he says. "Okay, I said my piece and wish you well Sean. I just hope I won't have to attend your funeral someday soon."

They went to the beach. Uncle Preston was in his early thirties, a little taller than him, with medium brown hair, and brown eyes. Sean can see a bit of chest hair sneaking out from behind Preston's tank top. He's in good shape -says he jogs a bit and likes the chest rowing machine at the gym. His hair is cut short.

77

Preston plays volleyball with the guys on the beach. He is an average player. He does miss a few volleys, and hits the sand. Sean has to laugh. He tries hard. As for Sean, he's too lethargic to play.

That night when Preston was asleep, he sneaked into the bedroom and steals forty dollars from his wallet, left out on the night stand.

The next day Preston happens to check his wallet to see if he has enough gas money for the car. It's an hour ride back to Orlando and he wants a full tank. What a surprise to find some of his money missing. He smacks his forehead with the palm of his hand and says, "How stupid of me to be so careless leaving my wallet exposed. Sean took it!"

He was waiting for Sean when he came out of the bedroom. As Sean gets closer, Preston punches him in the stomach. Falling to the floor, Preston's on top of him, pulling his hair. "Ouch, ouch, ouch!", he yells. "What's that for?"

"Sean, you took money out of my wallet during the night. That's what this is all about."

"No, I didn't", he lies.

There's more hair pulling and a smack across the face. "Don't lie to me, Sean. It's only me and you in the house."

"Maybe it fell out while at the beach."

"No, I know approximately how much I had, and now some of it is gone. Where is it?", he screams.

"I don't know, I don't know." he says.

Uncle Preston is smacking him on the face. He starts to crawl away towards the couch. Then Preston kicks him in the rear end - a maneuver his English cousins call the "Tower Hill play" - a kick in the ass and a slap across the face.

"You're a God damn thief Sean - a piece of shit, a piece of work. I'm glad your mother, my sister, is not here to witness this. Your grand parents didn't have to care for you. You could have been put into a foster home. But no, you had to steal from them too. Yes Sean, a real piece of work. I just lost all respect for you. Don't talk to me for the rest of my stay here. Get out of my sight."

Sean goes to his room and puts on the head phones to listen to music until he falls asleep. Uncle Preston is watching television in the living room. He doesn't want to see him either.

The next morning, Monday, Preston drops him off at high school. The silence on the ride over was heavy. As he gets out of the car, Preston said, "a piece of shit."

Sean stands at his locker waiting for Zack to come. There he is, coming down the hall with a huge crowd following him. There's still a chance the crowd might see Zack do his work, like punch face, kick ribs. Zack said, "Got my money?" Sean hands him the forty dollars stolen from him. He takes the money and with his other hand punches Sean once in the stomach. Down he crumbles lying on his stomach, thinking "when is all this punishment going to stop?"

As Zack towers over him, proclaiming to the crowd, "Look guys, I polished my boots this morning and I didn't have to scuff them up."

Sean opens his eyes and sees he's only inches from Zack's square toed boots. Yup, they were highly polished and the lights of the ceiling were sparking off the tips.

Everyone walked away. He's now the school's worst scumbag. No one is going to talk to him now. Feeling like a beaten puppy, he needed to smoke a joint.

Chapter 24

Black

When Sean starts to feel stressful at home, he would light up a joint. He kept a plastic bag of "stash" outside his bedroom window, hidden in the shrubbery, so grandpa wouldn't find it when mowing the lawn, which he was supposed to do, but never did lately. He'd climb in and out the window many times to have a puff outside, not wanting his bedroom to smell like a pungent reefer.

Grandpa was still yelling at him to pick up his clothes all around the bedroom. The bed was never made and it was always a rumpled mess. "God doesn't he ever stop", he says.

He got tired of hearing about his clothes, taking a pair of scissors and cutting them up into small pieces, and threw them into the laundry basket.

When Grandpa went to wash the clothes, he saw the laundry basket full of these cut fabrics. He said to Sean, "What's this?"

"Now you don't have to worry about my clothes on the floor", he said. "I don't have any more, just scraps and pieces."

"Don't expect grandma to buy you any more clothes. We

told you we couldn't afford some of this stuff you are costing us", grandpa said.

"I don't need them. I'll wear what I have on, stink or no stink", he said defiantly.

With that said, Sean stomped out of the house to the garage, takes hold of his bicycle, and sped off to one of his reefer buddies' house who has a car - a piece of junk, but it runs. He asks him to take him to the Mall near the Interstate.

Sean tells his buddy that he wanted some new clothes - the black stuff, like a tee shirt, pants and a belt. He was just going to steal them. His buddy wanted no part of this. He would just stay in the food court until Sean was done. Meanwhile, Sean had pocketed at the drugstore, black eye shadow, hair dye and black nail polish.

That night at home, he dyes his shag haircut black, and applies the black nail polish as best as he could. In the morning, he undertakes the black eye shadow in the bathroom mirror. Dressing in his new black "digs", he walks into the kitchen. Grandpa was reading the newspaper and drinking a cup of coffee at the kitchen table. He lifted his eyes and sat back looking at Sean over the top of his eyeglasses, then said, "If you think for one minute I'm going to drive you to school and let you get out of my truck looking like that, you can walk to school. I wouldn't want to be embarrassed that you're my grandson who looks like one of those weird, hippy-dippy rock stars."

Sean ran down to the school bus stop as quickly as he could, and got on the bus at the last minute. His fellow students looked at him strangely. In school, at the locker, he heard a trio of girls, walking by, saying, "Ever since Zack almost threw him down the stairs, he's been acting weird. He gives me the shivers."

Sean didn't care anymore. He'd show them, by sauntering down the hall giving "attitude". His school friends were avoiding him. Zack wouldn't even acknowledge him when passing in the hallways or even in the gym. He can't blame him after the hurt of his betrayal. On the school bus rides, no one would sit in the seat next to him, guessing he was too weird looking for them. He would just stare out the bus window as they drove along.

Sean was still smoking reefers, but not as much lately. Money was becoming scarce to buy a bag of weed, which was up to $60.00 per bag now. He mooched as much as possible from the boys behind the tennis bleachers. He was starting to isolate himself by not going to class, and did nothing extra, played no basketball and avoided going to gym classes as much as possible. He was weak and skinny and would look stupid in the showers with a head of black hair and light brown down below, knowing the guys couldn't wait to check him out and laugh.

The Sweetheart Dance was coming up. Everyone was talking about it. "Who was going with whom?" No girls were talking to him like they had before. He felt so left out, no part of anything.

The Sweetheart Dance was being held in the gymnasium with all the pink heart shaped trimmings inside. He bicycled over to the school that night, and stayed in the darkness of the parking spaces, he watched everyone going into the dance, dressed in their best clothes and hair combed certain ways. The boys were showing their best manners, escorting their dates. Every now and then, he'd catch a whiff of perfume, and could hear the band playing inside.

He puffed a few joints, sat on his bicycle watched the festivities, hearing the laughter and saw the good time his school friends were having. It made him feel not part of anything. A deep hurt developed in his heart, so painful he could hardly bear it. "What have I done to myself?" His eyes started to tear up. "I got to get out of here", he says.

He pedaled across town on his bicycle to an overpass of the Interstate Highway. Sean stopped near a railing and watched the headlights of the traffic below. He noticed the truck traffic was particularly heavy that night.

All he'd have to do is drop off the bridge right in front of an eighteen wheeler, and that would be it, he thought.

He screams as loud as he could, "No one cares - not even God! He hates me. I can't feel His love. Ahhhh!" Tears flow down his cheeks. The black mascara is running down in streaks. He looks like a ghoul.

"I hate myself! I hate myself!", he screams with his arms up in the air. "Ahhhh!"

He had been leaning forward on the bicycle pedals, so the motorists below could see his anguish. That's when he fell forward, and then everything went black.

Chapter 25

Bump

Sean sensed people moving around him. Then he opened his eyes to see a middle aged nurse with a ponytail, getting ready to wipe his dirty face with a damp cloth. He was lying down on something. His head was on a pillow.

"Where am I?" he asked.

"You're at the hospital emergency room. The ambulance brought you in about ten minutes ago. The policemen who found you said you had a nasty fall on the Interstate Bridge with your bike on top of you. You have a cut on your forehead which knocked you out." she said. "How are you feeling now?"

"I feel okay", he replies.

"The policeman found your school identity card in your pocket and has reached your grandparents. Do you live with them?", she asks.

"Yah, ever since I was a baby. My parents were killed in a car accident on the Interstate. Can I sit up?", he asks.

"No, just lie there a bit longer. The doctor may give request a CT scan, to see if there's any swelling or bleeding in the brain, or any cracks or structural damage to the skull. It was some nasty fall you sustained. The impact is a shock to your nervous system. Are you feeling any numbness or nausea?", the nurse asks.

"No."

"We have you hooked up to some monitors, taking your blood pressure and such, while you were unresponsive. I have to ask you a few questions to help the doctor in his examination of you. Have you smoked marijuana lately? The reason I ask you, is because the policemen found a lighter and reefer papers in your pocket."

"Yes, I had a few joints before going over to the interstate", he said.

"Any thoughts of suicide?"

"Yah, it passed through my mind at how convenient it would be with all the trucks below."

"Why Sean?", she asks.

"I guess I'm unhappy. I felt left out and no one loved me anymore. I just left the Sweetheart Dance at school and saw everyone having a good time. I look freaky and scary with this mascara running down my face. I hate what I have done to myself." He began to cry.

"You know Sean", she said. "Behind that black mask is a nice looking guy with a bright future ahead of him. All you've got to do is reach out and take it. You know sometimes God gives us a bump to get us to go in the right direction. Maybe, this is the bump you needed. Think about it. Is life that terrible?", she said.

He looked at her, but didn't say anything. Her statement got him thinking. "Yah it's time to make a change in my life", he says.

Just then, grandpa and grandma arrived. You could tell grandma had been crying and was very concerned about him. "Sean," she said, "are you okay? I was so worried when the hospital said you were hurt on the Interstate. All I could think of was your parents. I didn't want to lose you Sean. We love you." grandma said, as she wrapped her arms around him and gave him a big hug.

The doctor came over to examine him. He shined his little flashlight into his eyes, and gave him commands to test for the motor skills. He checked the monitors and had Sean stand up and walk around.

"Any dizziness? Do you feel light headed?", he asks.

"No, I feel alright. I just want to go home."

"Okay, have your grandparents sign these release forms and then you're free to go", he says.

Grandpa said, "C'mon son, it's time to go home."

As they were leaving, the nurse came up to Sean and said, "The policeman said your bike will be at the police station, and Sean, think about what I said, okay?"

"Thanks!", he yells back, as he was being wheeled out of the E.M into the dark night.

Chapter 26

Normal

On the drive back home from the hospital, Sean gave some thought as to what the nurse had said. "Why are you doing this to yourself? You have a bright future ahead of you. Why are you throwing it away? Why are you hurting yourself and all those people who love you?"

That night, he gathered some cleaning things grandma had around the house. He removed the black dye out of his hair, by using a paste of dandruff shampoo, baby shampoo and baking soda which he let stand on his dry hair for one half hour before washing it out. Now his short shag haircut looked decent. He used grandma's perfume to spray on his black finger nails, then rubbed hand cleaner gel on, and wiped it off with a paper towel. Next, he blow-dried his hair after he took a shower, and searched for some clothes to wear that he hadn't cut up. He found in his closet a pair of Khaki pants, and in a drawer, a striped tee-shirt.

Grandpa and grandma were surprised to see him so clean. They were sitting at the kitchen table. He wished them a "good morning", hugged grandma, and kissed grandpa on the side of the head.

Sean said to Grandpa, "After school, I'm going to apply for the busboy job at the Blue Tiki Restaurant. I heard they are hiring."

"That would be wonderful Sean", he said. After he left home for the school bus, grandpa walked down the hallway to his bedroom, and peeked in. The bed was made, and everything was picked up and put away. He returned to grandma and said, "I guess everything is back to normal. His room is clean and neat. I think he's back with us again."

Grandma said, "I prayed so hard for that boy. I just didn't want him to get hurt."

Later, grandpa heard her on the telephone making a hair appointment at the beauty salon, to have her hair done. It had been a long time since she had it styled. "Yes, everything is getting back to normal", he thought.

After being dropped off by the school bus after school, Sean walked over to the Blue Tiki. It had a massive thatched roof. He noticed the sign at the entrance that said "Happy Hour every day, and our Famous Lobster Bisque, a tourist delight."

He looked up inside at the roof when he went in, and saw the intricate weaving of the palm leaves on the open wood frame. It was a work of art.

The tables were covered with blue oil cloth coverings, with the seat cushions to match. The sea breezes were flowing through the place and you could see the whole marina and shoreline from inside.

The waitress brought the owner over - a short, plump Italian man, partially bald - to talk to him. He said, "I see you looking up at the thatched roof. Do you know how it was constructed?" Sean could see he wanted to talk about it.

"Sure." he said.

The owner explained how he wanted a tropical restaurant near the water. Someone suggested a thatched roof building.

He found out the county required no permits to build, as long as it was done by the Seminole Indians, the old fashion way, all hand tied. Historically, it was the only structure in Florida that would be left standing after a hurricane, before the state got populated. The Seminoles would select a local tree to cut for the framework, like beech wood, pine or palm wood. They would pre-cut everything, strip the bark off, and soak them in water. Lashings from the bark were used to hold the framework together. As the lashings dried, everything was pulled tighter. No bolts or nails would be used in the roof's construction.

Sean was hired to start the next day after school, with one day off on the weekends. He was given a white apron to wear, and the waitress explained what he had to do. He was a busboy, and had to clear the tables of dishes, wipe everything down, sweep and help waitresses as much as possible. He was so excited with his first job. Grandma made his favorite dinner the next night, lasagna, with pineapple upside down cake, to celebrate this big event in his life.

Once Sean had saved enough money from working at the Blue Tiki, he asked grandpa to drive grandma and him to the Mall. He stayed in the Food Court reading a newspaper and having coffee. Grandma did her browsing in all the stores, while Sean looked for a western clothing shop. He was looking for something special for Zack in the shirt racks. He wanted to be his friend once again, and needed a consolation gift to make this happen. He found a beige shirt with camouflage cuffs, collar and back yoke. Bone snaps were down the front, on the pockets and cuffs - just what he was looking for. It was a bit expensive, but not tawdry, so he bought it anyway. On the way to the check out counter, he found beige camouflaged framed sunglasses. Knowing Zack would love them as well, he had the salesgirl put them in the western logo bag with some colored tissue sticking out the top.

The next day in school, Sean walked down to Zack's hall locker. He was standing there ignoring him. He could see Zack peeking out the sides of his eyes looking at him.

"Zack, I bought you something", Sean said. He turned around and looked at him. He gave him the bag.

"It's for you, Zack. I want us to be friends again. I'm so sorry for all that's happening between us. Please take this gift."

Zack opens the bag and pulls out the shirt, holds it up and says "It's great Bro. I love it." He checks its size, and it's the right size too. He puts it on over his dark tee shirt and jeans.

"There's something else in the bag." Sean says.

Zack rummages around the bottom of the bag and finds the camouflaged sunglasses. He puts them on. He looks cool, wearing his favorite pattern, camouflage.

Zack grabs him and pulls him in for the big hug. Sean could feel his strong body against him. They pat each other on the back, thumping away.

"Hey Bro, you're my favorite Bud. I missed you so much this past year. I had no one to talk to. Yah, I talk to the girls, but it's not the same as sharing your feelings with a guy. Only they can understand what you're talking about. I'm sorry I called you a shithead. You know I don't like to swear. It makes you seem ignorant. I'm glad Mr. Crews stopped me from throwing you down the stairs. I would have hurt you badly. I've been going to church a lot, asking God to help me control my anger", Zack said.

Just then, the school bell rang. It was time to go to their homerooms.

"See me later, Sean!", Zack yells, going into his classroom. "We'll catch up at lunch time in the cafeteria."

Chapter 27

May

Cinco De Mayo Fiesta is held every year on the fifth of May. It's celebrated by the Mexican people throughout Florida - a day when they were liberated from foreign intervention in Mexico in 1862. It's like our 4th of July.

The tall water tower with "Welcome to Pepper Beach" painted on its side, can be seen from the Interstate Highway. This is where the poor section of town begins. It's called "Tommy Town" after some guy named Thomas who brought up all the dilapidated houses and shacks, and rented them to the Mexicans. Some Mexicans consider these run-down homes better than what they left behind. At least they have running water and electricity, a free clinic and free education for their children.

Every year, grandpa loved to go to the festival. He loved Mexican food. Grandma says it's okay. She liked the bowl of beans with a mild salsa on it. Sean can't stand the smell of the condiment cumin. To him it smells like dirty socks. He settled for a burrito and a slice of pina (pineapple) from a small taqueria. Picnic tables are set up in different areas for people to enjoy their meals. The Mexican men wore white sombreros and guayabera shirts with pleats in the back. The musicians were playing their big guitars, called guitarrons (a heavy instrument with a "v" back for deep tones, used in traditional mariachi music). A strap was over their shoulders holding it up.

The Peruvian immigrants played their pan pipe flutes, called "zampona". It's an ancient musical instrument of five tubes made of wood. It's considered a sacred sound from God. The sound is eerie to Sean. They had their display tables set up and sold their music disks.

They took it all in while walking the street - the smells, the noise, and crying children who have the biggest dark eyes Sean has ever seen. They were so beautiful.

The main street is called "Calle De Milargos", Street of Miracles. On both sides of the street are Mexican businesses. Irene's Tienda, sold boots, hats and clothing. Next is Juan's Barber Shop. Then there is Pequeno's Restaurant, a Mexican Mercado, coin laundry, and Pedro's Thrift Store.

Sean went into the Mexican market to see what kind of food they sold. One wall had wooden trays filled with bananas, tomatoes, onions, peppers, and corn. In front of that, was a low glass top ice cream cooler with ice cream sandwiches, and several flavors of ice pops on a stick. He saw a lot of young people walking around eating their ice creams. On another wall was a glass encased meat case with blocks of cheese, lunch meat, fried chicken and a tray of cows' tongues. They were larger than he ever imagined. The store had stacks of tortilla shells and corn husks. At first, Sean didn't know what corn husks were for. Then later he saw them being soaked in water and wrapped around tamales before being cooked - this keeps the flavor in. The husks are then stuffed with vegetables and meat.

He got a bottle of soda, called Zap. There was another soda called Hug. All the sodas were bottled in Mexico.

Inside, the smell of fried chicken permeated the air. The wood platform was piled high with 25 pound bags of rice and beans. Gallon jugs of cooking oil were displayed nearby. "No wonder these people are getting fat", he thought.

Leaving the market, he noticed two small covered cookers near the cashier. One pot said "Cajun", and the other, "Original". He took the cover off one to peek inside and caught a whiff of boiled peanuts simmering in a dark brown liquid. Neither the smell nor the looks were appealing to Sean. Nearby was "Barbacoa De Cabeza" (Barbecue Head of Cow).

At the end of the street is Santa Rosa Church, a one story white wooden building with a high pitched roof with a small gold cross on the peak. The double wood front doors were carved by Mexicans, with a rose in the top panel, and a cross in the bottom panel. The door had banged metal hinges and hand-pulls.

To the right of the entrance, was a white statue of Jesus with His hands held down and palms out, as if He was welcoming the people. The statue is lit at night. On the other side of the front door is a single flag pole displaying the Florida State flag, and below it, a fluttering flag of Mexico. The front doors were outlined with a garland of natural native flowers and Florida holly, now known as Florida's native pepper plant.

Sean tells grandma he's going inside the church. She tells him to look for them at the beer wagon. Grandpa likes Modelo Beer, and she'll settle for Corona.

The church was small with simple little white lights along the upper nave in the apse behind the altar. The apse was painted sky blue with a hint of clouds. A huge crucifix made from timbers, was suspended over the altar. It looked like it was floating in the sky. Sean took a seat to the left. A niche with the Virgin Mary, is on the right side. At the base of the statue is a bunch of roses. The altar was draped with native flowers indigenous to the area, with fan palms and small branches. It was quite lovely. He looked up at the suspended crucifix - the Spanish wood carvers knew how to depict the agony of Christ in their woodwork.

Sean sat there thinking, "How could a mortal man submit to this pain to save our souls - were we worth it?" He kept looking at Him, his eyes became moist. He found it hard to keep his eyes on the carved agony of Christ. "My God I'm sensitive to this." he thought.

Sean knelt down, lowered his head and said a little prayer, then sat back humbly in the pew until he felt a peacefulness come over him. "I'll be okay God." he said to himself, getting up and departing the church, feeling very happy and contented.

He found grandma and grandpa at one of the drinking tables. Grandma asked, "Are you alright Sean?"

"Yes grandma, I feel great." Grandpa wanted to check more of the vendors' tables. Maybe he could find the part he was looking for amongst the junk and Spanish artifacts. Grandma was busy at a separate table and then at the Mexican shawl display. She finally settled for a colorful shawl to put over herself while watching television at home, with little Puffy on her lap.

Grandpa had enough, and announced it was time to go home. They walked down a newly paved side street, to grandpa's pickup truck.

The houses were painted bright orange, or blue, or green. Small chickens with red feathers on the bottom, and black feathers on their neck and head, ran around pecking at everything. Oh! The dogs, plenty of them about, were licking themselves you know where, probably from the fleas. "How disgusting", thought Sean.

They almost passed a Mexican farmer and his family selling their vegetables on the side of the road. Grandma had grandpa pull over. Sean got out with grandma, and marveled at the huge onions, as big as grapefruits. The carrots, cucumbers, heads of lettuce, and cantaloupe, were all huge.

"Buenos dias", said Sean to the teenage daughter.

She replied "Gracias muchacho." and waited on grandma, to fill her bags. They bought enough vegetables to eat for a week.

On the ride back home, Sean informed grandpa and grandma, "You know, the Spanish people are hard workers. They keep their children clean and make sure they go to school. They're so proud of their children being Americans, just like we are. Gracias Dios mio."

Chapter 28

Preston

Sean had been saving his money from working at the Blue Tiki Restaurant, for the past month, knowing he had to make amends with Uncle Preston for stealing his money. He put the forty dollars he had stolen from him, in an envelope, along with a letter of apology:

Dear Uncle Preston,

Here's the forty dollars I took from you. I know I hurt you and you lost trust in me. I want us to be friends again. I want to go canoeing once more and listen to your stories of the land, water and animals. I always enjoyed these times. Can we do it again? I'm sorry for what I did.

Your nephew,
Sean

Sean put everything into an envelope and mailed it to Uncle Preston in Orlando.

A few weeks later, Uncle Preston called him, and said he

could get some day passes to Underground Disney. "Do you want to go?"

"Yes of course", was the reply.

"Then clear it with your boss at the restaurant, get a bus ticket, and I'll meet you at the bus terminal in Orlando this Friday", Preston said.

Sean had grandpa drive him to the bus pickup point at a gas station on the corner of Cracker Highway and Main Street. Uncle Preston met Sean at the Orlando bus stop an hour later. They went right to his apartment across the street from Lake Eola, in the center of Orlando.

Sean had never been to Preston's apartment. This was a new and exciting experience for him. Preston lived on the sixth floor, just above the treetops. From the balcony, they could see the whole lay out of Lake Eola Park and the walkway around the lake, with white swan pedal boats floating down below.

The one bedroom apartment was quite large. The living room had white walls with a few framed prints of architectural interests. The ceiling to floor sliding glass doors at one end were protected with big bamboo roll up shades. Here, Preston kept his drafting table with an attached lamp, rolls of blueprint material on top, and a wicker basket on the floor, with more tubes of paper. It looked busy.

The place was sparsely furnished. Along one wall was a long dark burgundy couch with big pillows. "This is where you sleep." he said. On the opposite side was a big television screen hung on the wall with a low chest of drawers underneath, piled high with books and magazines. Two upholstered chairs with a burgundy and white pattern, flanked the chest. The dining table was black with four matching chairs, and there was a black coffee table in front of the couch, and two side tables with lamps.

The bedroom was painted a chocolate brown with a low modern bed, no headboard, all done in a dark fabric ensemble with big pillows to match. Uncle Preston calls this his "man cave". The window was covered in a blackout drapery. In the corner was a chair piled high with clothes and a laundry basket next to it, and a floor lamp.

"Hey Preston!", Sean yelled out. "I see you have the same laundry basket as me and the same color too."

"Yah, we both got the same gift from grandpa", said Preston. "You know how he is - so neat and tidy."

"He loves doing laundry and taking care of the house. I guess that's from the years of being organized as a mechanic up at the car dealership on Main Street", said Sean.

A six-drawer chest was opposite the bed, with an old-world conquistador map of Florida on the wall, next to Preston's old University of Florida's gator shirt - blue with a big green gator head on it - stuck to the wall with stickpins.

"Ae you hungry?" asked Preston. "Let's walk down Orange Avenue to this little restaurant I know of. Once I park my car, I don't like moving it, because someone always will take the spot, and then I have to drive around until I find another empty space. It's so time consuming."

After dinner, Sean walked around Lake Eola with Uncle Preston, who explained everything about it. At one end was an amphitheater with weekend musical shows. The fountain in the middle of the lake is illuminated with different changing colors, as it shoots a jet stream of water high into the air. At the other end of the lake was a red pagoda, a confederate soldier statue, and flower gardens. There were plenty of ducks around, preening their feathers, along with beautiful black swans patrolling the shoreline. The walkways were busy with people walking around. Lovers and rollerbladers were everywhere. It was so magical. No wonder the tourists love visiting here, as Sean has just found out.

Back at the apartment, they sat on the balcony and watched the city lights illuminate with the ever-changing colored lights of the fountain. Sean was glad to be back in Uncle Preston's favor once again.

Sean noticed a small picture of himself, on the bedroom dresser, from when he was nine years old. He was holding a large paddle next to a canoe, squinting, because the sun was in his eyes. He thought to himself, "I had forgotten that Uncle Preston had taken this picture of me on one of our canoeing trips. I guess he thought enough of me, to frame and display it." There were other pictures - one of grandma and grandpa, and another of Preston dressed up in a shirt and tie with Minnie Mouse and Mickey Mouse standing on each side of him.

Chapter 29

Disney

They drive to Disney World early the next morning then stopped at a fast food restaurant for an egg and bacon sandwich. Sean got orange juice, and Preston, coffee with one sugar and one milk. Sean was always amazed how people are very fussy about their coffees. Grandpa and Uncle Preston like their coffee the same way, grandma on the other hand likes her coffee with two sugars and two milks. When she came out of her bedroom in the morning, there was Puffy following with tail up and meowing all the way to the back door, which grandma opens to let her out to do her cat thing. Grandpa has grandma's coffee ready for her on the kitchen table. They sip their coffee slowly, not saying a word to each other. They don't have to. They understand each other very well.

They arrived in back of the Disney complex in a large parking lot. The two large tunnel entrances to underground Disney are straight ahead. Uncle Preston showed the guard their two passes to take the tour. They are issued name tags and a golf cart to drive the massive, irregular shaped circle tunnel under Disney World. Overhead were lots of pipes on the ceiling, one for electricity, some for water, painted blue, and a 20" diameter pipe for trash removal, which is pumped behind Stone Mountain and recycled. Disney is big on staying green. The walls of the tunnel were color coded with different signs for what's above, in the tourist area.

Disney couldn't build their fun complex underground because of the water seepage, so the cement tunnel was built above ground and covered over with tons of dirt from the large lagoon they made in the center of Magic Kingdom. The slight incline is not noticed by the tourists.

Preston waved to a few people he knew, as he explained to Sean how it all works. They passed rooms filled with uniforms the employees wear, costume rooms, wigs, some weighing 35 pounds each, dresses and all things needed to make Disney the happiest place to be on earth. There was even a hair salon, a bank and an employee's cafeteria with prices for food cheaper than above. All foods are prepared in the tunnel and lifted to the restaurants overhead.

It's funny to see Mickey Mouse walking down the hall with his costume head in his hand and half a Pluto eating in the cafeteria. When above, every actor in costume must play their part to the fullest.

Preston took Sean to the costume room of Minnie and Mickey Mouse. There is a small girl suiting up in Mickey's costume. She told them it doesn't matter if a girl or boy plays Mickey or the other small Disney characters. The costume is determined by the physical size of the actor inside.

The costumes are bulky and hard to maneuver in. They're smelly from sweat, as it's hot inside of them. The plaster heads are musty inside and they look through slits in the cheeks. They're brought up topside on an elevator, perform in front of the tourists for 15 minutes with a handler nearby holding radio devices in case of trouble, then brought back down for 45 minutes to recover by taking the head gear off. The girl actor informed Preston and Sean that they can't be claustrophobic. You must keep your control at all times. Once you're zipped into your costume, it could be a bit scary. She told them of a new girl who got zipped into her costume, after a few minutes became frightened, and started screaming. The handler had to get her behind the secret door really quickly and unzip her. The girl was so scared, she gathered up her things from her locker and quit.

Little Mickey told them how she got kicked, pushed, and punched by the kids. She said she even gets groped by the men and sometimes by women. They all think a man is in the Mickey costume. You never know who plays the part she said.

After a few hours of touring in the underground, they went to eat in the employee's cafeteria. Then Preston took Sean to his workspace in a glass building near the entrance to Disney World. He showed Sean his drafting station and something he was working on. Sean realized he was involved in all phases of designing the Disney Complex. That's how Preston knew so much about everything. Sean was very proud of his uncle, the designer draftsman.

"I can get you a job here when you graduate." Preston said. "That's if you want it."

They spent most of the day at Disney. Then it was time to go back to Preston's apartment.

Preston parked the car in a space they found near his apartment, and walked down to Orange Avenue, to find a place to eat. After dinner they took a side street near the city library to Lake Eola. The fountain was constantly changing colors, and the jet stream of water was being color illuminated also. Music was being pumped through the speakers, hidden in the trees. They walked around the lake once more, and had fun watching the people. Some were rollerblading, others were feeding the ducks from the machines they fed money into for the feed. Everyone seemed happy.

Preston and Sean went back to the apartment and sat on the balcony. Sean drank a soda, and Preston a beer. Little by little, the lights of Orlando were being lit. It was so magical. Sean was enthralled. He can see why Preston chose to live here. Sean thought, "It's a shame I have to leave tomorrow. I want to stay forever."

Chapter 30

Visit

Sean was sitting in the living room with grandpa, watching television. Grandma, as usual, was in her bedroom watching her favorite television shows. She had told Sean that she never liked the shows grandpa was interested in, and she hated football season, calling it an intrusion into the household. She said she didn't mind football games, but wouldn't sit in all night, seven days a week, watching every football game to be found. Grandpa was like that.

There was a knock at the door. Sean got up to see who it was. He opened the door and there was Adam, standing with a sheepish grin on his face. Sean had not thought of, or seen Adam in over half a year. "He should be with me in our senior year", Sean thought.

"Hey Buddy, how's it going?", Sean greeted Adam. "Come in. Let me see you. Grandpa, look who's here. It's Adam." Grandpa grunted and bobbed his head up and down. He was too absorbed in his football games to say hello.

Adam asked, "Can we go for a walk and talk?"

Sean replied, "Sure, we can walk down to the beach and

sit under one of the pavilions looking at the ocean. So what gives Adam?", Sean asked.

"Well, you know I've been gone for over half a year. They sent me to Tallahassee for some treatments. I worked with the therapist to get to the bottom of my problem. I had a private room, clean uniforms and clean sheets. The food wasn't bad. My parents were allowed to come up and visit me twice a month for 1 hour, then they had to leave until the next visit.

My problem was, and you don't know this, but I fell in love with David, my dentist. We had a relationship for almost a year. I felt I was part of his family, as his wife and kids were so accepting of me in their home. I felt I belonged there."

"When David told me he was moving out west and I was no longer going to be part of the family, I started to lose it. Then when he backed out of his deal to give me the five acres he promised, I wanted to hurt him as much as he had hurt me. I felt used and betrayed. So I freed his horses from the stables and burned it down instead. I also burned my horse too, which would have been a reminder of David, had it lived. Then I lost it, went berserk and was committed. I didn't know I was like this. He took advantage of my sensitivity and played on it. I was so vulnerable at that age. I wanted to love and be loved. It just so happens it was the wrong person." Adam took a long pause. "Got a cigarette?"

"No I don't smoke anymore. I used to smoke marijuana when you were away.", Sean replied.

"That's okay.", Adam said. "I just need a little something.", he continued. "I just want to go on and tell you what it was like. My mind went into a dark place. The doctors thought I was at the edge of madness, but the mind wants to survive too. I was in a large black space, somewhere in my skull, like a little grain of sand.

I sat with my knees drawn up to my chin. I stayed sitting

there for some time in the blackness, trying to sort things out, and became aware of my own senses.

A small beam of light appeared. I watched it for some time. Then it got bigger. I heard a voice saying, "Adam, Adam".

The next time I heard my name, "Adam, Adam", I went to the light and put my finger into the beam then withdrew it quickly. I didn't want to get hurt. Later I heard my name again, and I put my arm into the light. It felt warm and good. Then I withdrew my arm. I waited a while, thinking what I should do next. I finally stepped fully into the light and looked down and saw my bare feet under a white gown. My hair was long and limp, and covering my face. As I looked up, I felt okay and safe. I stayed in that position for some time, enjoying the light and warmth. Then Bham!

I opened my eyes to see a middle-aged nurse over me who wiped my brow with a damp towel."

"Adam, Adam, are you okay?", she asked. "I came every day and said your name with the hope you would come out of your coma. Do you want anything?"

"Sean, do you know what I asked for? A hamburger. She laughed, and I laughed, with all kinds of tubes in me and bags of fluids on the side.

The doctor was called in, looked into my eyes with his little flashlight, and looked at the machines monitoring me, and said it was okay to let me loose.

The next day I started my therapy sessions to get to the bottom of what drove me to this emotional state. I knew soon I would be on the road to recovery."

"You know, Adam, I had no idea what had happened to you", Sean informed him. "Rumors were flying around, but no one knew of your love relationship. Are you okay with yourself now?", he asked.

"Yes, I can handle what I am. I'm not afraid anymore. I just wanted to tell you."

Adam continues talking to Sean about another young teenager he accompanied to the therapy sessions. His name was Phillip, and had been there longer than Sean. He had severe issues with his step-mother who had married his biological father after his mother's death.

She had locked him in his bedroom for four years, because she disliked him. Phillip never understood the contempt, yet, she treated her own son like gold. He was the same age as Phillip and witnessed the beatings, the head smashing with the wood cutting board, and other hurtful things. He showed no concern, being glad it wasn't him.

In the beginning of the marriage, Phillip was placed in a large dog cage as punishment. Growing bigger, the step-mother locked him in his bedroom, devoid of electronics, paper, pencil and television. Somehow, he managed to entertain himself with an old Lego set and a mound of clay. He used his imagination to create robot figures, especially the warrior types.

For breakfast, she served him a bowl of dry cereal with a smidgen of milk, and peanut butter sandwiches, an apple and crackers for lunch at school. No milk or juice was provided. Phillip had to drink water only.

She would be waiting for him when he returned home from school, to do his chores.....like clean the house, mow the lawn, and dispense the litter from the kitty boxes for her nine cats. If it wasn't to her liking, the way he did these things, he'd get slammed into the wall or hit in the head with a pot or pan, leaving a permanent lump in the back of the head. He never cried out - just took the abuse. He was thrown into his bedroom for the rest of the day, with the step-mother latching the door shut from the outside.

When his father was home from his long truck driving

trips, she served him a great meal with the two boys present. If Phillip dared to complain, the next day he would get a beating. His father never commented on how he was treated. What a wuss! Everything had to appear normal. These were the times Phillip ate well and was able to play with his step-brother.

Growing older, taller and stronger, Phillip started to resist, only to get slammed down. One day, he finally had taken enough abuse. He smashes the bedroom door down and attacks his step-mother, knocking her down with his fists and kicking her unconscious. His rage was uncontrollable. The police were summoned and his parents committed him to Tallahassee to help control his belligerence."

Adam said he could hear Phillip down the hall in his room, screaming out "I hate her! I hate her! I hate her!", then he would lower his head and race into the wall to render himself senseless.

Adam said to Sean "I felt no threat from Phillip, but it became a bit scary at times. He knew from the therapy sessions, it would take Phillip a long time to recover from the shackling, and become normal again."

"Thanks for telling me all this, Adam", Sean said. He put his arm around his shoulders. They sat quietly for a long time, looking out at the ocean, not saying anything.

Sean kept thinking how nice it was to be back with an old friend, who had been through a terrible experience. Soon, they would be graduating and getting on with their lives.

Chapter 31

Cooking Class

It was the first day of their senior year, and it was Registration Day. They had to select the classes they wanted for the rest of the year.

Adam and Sean were at one end trying to decide what subjects they needed to take. Zack pushed his way through the crowd to reach them.

"Hey guys", he shouts.

Papers in hand, Sean and Adam looked towards Zack, and simultaneously ask "What? What do you want?"

"Guys, take a cooking class with me." Zack exclaims.

"Why?", they question simultaneously.

"A girl I like just signed up for the class. I want to be her partner, but I don't want to do it alone. I need a masculine presence there", Zack answered.

"Why us?", Adam asked.

"Hey, you're my buds. It's only two days a week, last class on Tuesday and Thursday. It will be great, and lots of fun. Besides, guys should know how to cook nowadays.", answered Zack.

"Yah, you're right. I don't know a darn thing about cooking.", Sean said. "Do you Adam?"

"Not really." answers Adam. "But I should know."

They didn't know what the future held. Adam and Sean signed up for the cooking classes with Zack.

The teacher said she is very pleased the boys were taking an interest in cooking, as it was rare for boys to sign up.

Zack's smile was a mile long, as he returned to the girl that made eyes at him. He told her that he and she would be partners during the class.

The cooking class was held on the back side of the cafeteria, sharing a common wall of refrigerators and freezers. The ceilings were high, with big windows. Small tables were set up at the other end. Down the middle of the space, were two sheet metal tables with six stools on each side, for the twelve students per class. One table was for cutting, the other has many sinks for washing and cleaning up. In the middle of each table was a shelf separating each side, stacked with knives, spoons, and metal bowls.

Every student was issued a long blue apron. Girls and boys with long hair had to wear hair nets. Sean said "Thank God that I got my hair cut short." Adam also had his hair cut short too.

On the side wall, were the six double ovens with four burners on top of each, and a microwave oven overhead.

The teacher had a large blackboard on wheels, to chalk out what they were cooking, and other instructions for the day. There were also aluminum shelves on wheels, stacked with every pot and pan they would need for cooking, with metal spoons, strainers, more knives and such.

For the next few months they learned how to grill, bake, broil, steam, sauté, fry, blacken, brea, meuniere (dredging in flour), and bonne femme (home style cooking).

Sean and Adam were a team. Adam seemed to really catch on quickly, what to do, and what spices to use. Sean followed his lead. Sean thought Adam was good at everything he did.

Zack was busy down at his end of the table with his (so called) new girlfriend. She was infatuated with him. Zack talked constantly as they prepared the class meal from the mobile blackboard.

At the end of class, the students sampled each other's cooking. Sometimes teachers and school staff would also come by at the end of class to sample the student's experiments. Sean was informed by the janitor that their left-over pot roast was very good.

Near the end of the semester, the teacher surprised the class by bringing in a chef from an elegant Disney hotel. Chef Sammy Young, who worked at the Japanese restaurant atop one of the largest hotels in Disney. Chef Young was dressed in his white round chef's hat, chef's jacket and dark pants. He showed the class his personal set of knives made in Japan by a company that also made Samurai Swords. "Every good chef should have his own personal set of knives.", he said.

A student questioned "What part of Japan are you from?"

"I am from Brooklyn. I graduated from the New York City Culinary Institute. I had a propensity for throwing knives as a boy", he replied. He went on to share, that the Japanese restaurant hired him upon graduating, due to the fact that he looked Asian, and could do knife tricks as he prepared the meals for the tourists, adding that, the restaurant paid him well and the tourists' tips were extremely generous. "Oh by the way, I'm Korean," he said, "but the tourists didn't know. We all look the same to them." Chef Sammy laughed and the class laughed with him.

In the corner of the cooking space there is a small kitchen set up, used as a demo area, where Chef Sammy Young demonstrated and prepared his classic Asian dishes. His arms were a blur, as he tossed the knives around, sliced onions in midair, shouted his Korean slurs and made the most of his art. The students thoroughly enjoyed the demonstration. Sean thought to himself, "No wonder the tourists loved him. The class certainly did too."

There were cameras mounted above the demo area to show what the chef was doing, or the students could stand back and watch it on a flat screen television mounted on the wall.

All the students and teachers were given a small bowl of Chef Sammy's Asian cuisine, consisting of vegetables, sesame seeds, ginger, beef and noodles, sautéed in a butter teriyaki sauce.

Chef Sammy informed them, "Hey kids, I don't speak Japanese, only Korean. Again, what do the tourists know?" He put his hands together and bowed. The students returned the bow.

The end of the semester was fast approaching, and the teacher informed the class that there was going to be an Award of Excellence, given. Students could choose a category to display their talents.

Sean and Adam chose desserts, and decided they would do something fantastic.

When Sean got home, he ran down the street to his French neighbor Virgene's home, to ask her for something special to bake. "The French know how to cook", he thought, as he headed towards his neighbor house. Virgene and her husband were from Algiers. They chose Pepper Beach to reside because it reminded them of their small seaside village on the Mediterranean Sea, in Algiers on the North African coast.

Virgene was as tall as Sean, slender with medium brown hair brushed back, and held in place with a rhinestone clip barrette. Her eyes were brown and rouge is on her cheeks. She dressed in the smartest flat footwear, dark capris pants, and a white over blouse with dabs of ice cream colors on it. Her smile was resplendent as she spoke to Sean. "For you boys, let's see, something easy to make, that can't be messed up. Okay, I've got it: 'gateau au chocolat'. In other words, a chocolate cake said in French", she said.

Virgene wrote the recipe on a small card and handed it to Sean. He thanked her excitedly and then ran off to the grocery store to purchase the ingredients for the cake, aside from the fresh raspberries and whipped cream that were to be Adam's contribution.

In the classroom, Sean and Adam baked the cake in two round pans. They prepared a semi sweet chocolate cream spread to put between the layers, after cooling. The top was dusted with powdered sugar, and a double ring of fresh raspberries were placed along the edge. It looked beautiful, light and flavorful, with a tart raspberry and chocolate taste. "Voila" claimed Sean, upon completion.

The school photographer was there that day, taking pictures. Adam and Sean carefully held their cake up, and smiled as their picture was taken.

A short time later it was revealed that Sean and Adam had won the Award of Excellence for their dessert. The judges, teachers and staff were pleased with the taste and appearance. The picture of the boys grinning with their award-winning cake, was placed in the yearbook.

At first, it was hard for Sean to believe that they had achieved it, but then everybody loves red raspberries and chocolate cake - right?

Chapter 32

Tara

At the beginning of senior year, Sean noticed that there was a new girl a few lockers down from him.

He walked over to her and said "Hi, my name's Sean."

"Hi, I'm Tara."

"You're new to this school. I haven't seen you around before."

"I attended private school for the first three years. Then my parents wanted me to consummate my senior year in a public high school, for more real life experiences", she said.

"Maybe I'll see more of you about campus", Sean said as the first bell rang warning the students to get to their homerooms.

Tara had long thick dark hair that cascades down her shoulders erupting in a flurry of curls. Her eyes are dark and she was wearing the reddest of lipstick. She was a bit smaller than Sean. She wore a light blue peasant blouse with ribbon ties at her neck, a dark short skirt above the knees, along with fancy cowgirl boots with tassels in the front. She exuded a bubbly personality, which Sean liked. "She was HOT", he thought. Even some of his buddies thought Tara was attractive.

As the weeks flew by, Sean got to know Tara better. They exchanged pleasantries every day at her locker, yet she was not in any of his classes.

One day she approached Sean's locker and asked if he would like to attend her family's annual pig roast.

"Pretty sure I would love to", he answered, as she handed him a piece of paper with her telephone number, and directions on how to get to her family's horse ranch. Sean was so excited. "A date with a beautiful girl", he thought.

He swapped a Saturday with another busboy at the Blue Tiki, and asked grandpa to drive him out to the ranch north of town, the following Saturday morning.

Grandpa and Sean finally found her street, Pony Path Trail, a narrow road barely wide enough for two cars to pass each other. They passed a small ranch with a sign out front: "Alpacas, The Bad Boys of Pepper Beach" For Sale. Grandpa and Sean laughed. Grandpa said, "You got to be careful with those guys. They like to spit at you." Sean found the alpacas kind of funny looking with their sleepy eyes, chewing cud.

Across the street, a hay farmer with his big green machine, was rolling bales of hay, and leaving them scattered around the field for pick up the next day. The street was bordered on both sides with very old oak trees. The branches were thick with green moss and ferns growing on top. Spanish moss, four feet long, was hanging down like an old man's whiskers. The branches canopied the streets for a few miles. Through the trees, they saw Tara's sprawling house, set back about 1000 feet. The house had dormers on the roof, and was painted yellow with white trim and green shutters.

A great pasture was out front, with a dozen grazing horses. Two of them were mares with young colts which pranced about. As far as they could see, were pastures with horses.

To the left of the house they saw a large metal barn - the green metal roof was topped with a cupola.

Tara instructed them, on her note, to drive through the stone columns with horse statues on top, and the gates topped with brass finials.

The driveway was paved, and curved past the house to the back area. Each side of the driveway was fenced, and had pink crepe myrtle bushes planted as a border. They were in full bloom - a beautiful hot pink. Starlings were walking in a somewhat straight line, moving across the grass area, as they searched for bugs. This reminded Sean of a small army on maneuvers, with one chunky blackbird tagging along.

As grandpa approached the stables in his truck, Tara came out to greet them. Sean jumped out of the truck and introduced her to grandpa. As grandpa was getting ready to back up onto the pavement, he told Sean to call him when he was ready to come home.

Tara looks so pretty with her hair in a ponytail under her black fedora hat. She had her red and yellow shirt tucked into her dark jeans. Tara guided Sean over to where her parents were sitting, and introduced them. Tara looked like her mother, with dark hair and eyes. Her father was a head taller, with silver white hair under his dove-colored Stetson, and had a tan.

Then Tara asked, "Are you ready to go riding?"

"Only if you're not going to do anything crazy", replied Sean.

"Silly boy, don't be scared. I won't do anything crazy."

Tara led Sean into the twenty-stall barn, selecting a horse, and showed him how to install the bridal, the blanket and saddle.

They mounted the horses, and slowly they rode out of the barn along the white four rail fence to the end of the pasture area. They followed a path through the sawgrass along the lake, which was overflowing from previous heavy rains the day before.

The lake was long and narrow. In the distance, at the far end you can see dark strands of Sago Palms and Sabal Palmettos along with hedge-like clumps of Brazilian pepper trees and blankets of Spanish moss hanging everywhere.

Sean heard an osprey giving his shrill call for a mate, on the other side of the lake. The osprey had built a large nest of branches from twigs and other debris that he found in the area. He was high in the trees which gave him an unobstructed view of the lake. Sean watched as the osprey leapt out of his nest, whistling frantic notes as he swooped down ever so gracefully, his wings outstretched with little tip feathers sticking up in the air gliding his descent downward, making all the adjustments necessary to angle himself correctly to snag a six inch fish out of the water. Then there was a tremendous effort of flapping his wings to gain altitude, slowly turning around in a circle to make it back to his nest. He hovered above his nest flapping his wings furiously to slow down, and lightly touched down on the edge of the nest. No chicks were visible. Sean watched as the osprey ripped the fish apart, holding it down with one claw, and ate it.

Sean was wearing his dark baseball cap and big aviator sunglasses. He and Tara put suntan lotion on their faces, neck and arms, in the stables. He loved smelling the scent of coconut oil on his skin, as they rode in the sunshine.

Sean could feel the movement of the horse's muscles on the inner part of his leg, through his jeans. He enjoyed the ambling pace the horses set through the open fields before them.

The land was flat and quiet. Only the buzzing of bugs was evident. Slowly they rode in a circle and started to return to the ranch. In the tall sawgrass Tara pointed out an old faded red pickup truck. "Oh, that's been here for years", she said. The truck had big round fenders and bullet shaped headlights.

Sean suggested they go check it out. He got off his horse

and pushed through the tall grass, and pulled the door open with a groan and screech from the rusted hinges.

"Let's get inside", she suggested.

"Okay." Sean slid in behind the wheel and acted like a race car driver.

Tara slid in next to him. The seat was long and rigid with splits showing the stuffing peeking out, and the shift was on the floor with a white ball knob on top.

"Can you drive a stick shift?", she asked.

"No, I haven't got my license yet."

Tara leaned over and kissed Sean. Sean got a peculiar warm feeling. The two made out for ten minutes, then Tara said, "Let's take our tops off." Their bodies were pressed together, and again Tara spoke: "Let's take our bottoms off too." Sean became very excited, as a feeling came over him that he had never experienced before. He was surprised how smoothly he slid inside of her with the help of her hand. She felt so warm, and he loved the scent of her perfume. It was instinctive - he just knew what to do. They laid side by side for some time, Sean rubbing the skin on her back and buttocks. He felt wonderful - so grand, like nothing he had ever experienced before, as if he was in a dream world. He felt the warmth of her arms around him, drawing him closer. She finally sat up and said, "We'd better get back to the picnic before my parents wonder what happened to us." They got dressed and Sean reached for her hand as they ambled over to the horses grazing nearby.

Mist was starting to rise from the lake as the cool water was starting to grow warm from the sun.

They follow the path along the lake. They heard one of her cousins playing his guitar softly, and saw the sunlight rippling on the surface of the water. Deer were grazing on the far side of the lake with a pair of blue herons and a high stepping long legged egret, fishing for their next meals.

Slowly they walked the horses inside the stable. Tara showed Sean how to take the saddle off and place everything in its proper section. They rubbed down the horses with a dry towel, and put them each into their own stalls with fresh hay and water.

"I guess they're ready to serve the pig", Tara said. The two walked over to the table and filled their plates with food, and found a bench to sit on, their knees touched. They looked at each other and smiled. They now had a big secret.

Chapter 33

Hogs

Zack usually never talks much about his Dad. Sometimes after he comes back from visiting him at his crummy trailer, he would be "all wound up" about some hunting trip his uncle and dad had taken him on in the Ocala National Forest.

"During deer hunting season", Zack would say, "you're allowed one kill - one buck. Sometimes we go to Hog Island Park on the Withlacoochee River in Nobleton, or over to the St. John's River, north of Lake Monroe. That area is loaded with hogs. On one of our hunting trips, my father said I didn't know how to shoot a gun. He was right." Zack had never shot a gun before. "When a hog charged us once, I picked up the rifle, aimed and shot the beast right between the eyes. It was a lucky shot, an unbelievable shot. I dropped to my knees in disbelief. "Wow! Did you see that?" my uncle said. "Of course, you know that will never happen again." My dad just shook his head and said "You know son, if you were willing to kill an animal, you better be prepared to eat it." I never forgot that lesson. That's why there's so much wild meat in the freezer. "Ya know guys, someday I'm going to have you over for a cook out so you can savor my delectable delights", Zack said.

Adam and Sean looked at each other thinking, "How are we going to get out of this one?"

"Zack, you know we are not wild meat eaters. We'd rather have a hamburger instead", Sean said as he pointed to Adam and himself.

"You don't know what you will be missing", Zack says.

A few weeks later, Zack requests that they go on a hog hunt with him and Uncle Matthew, named after a disciple of Christ, by his religious mother.

Matthew was Zack's father's older brother. He had never married and had served two tours of duty in the Marine Corps. At one time, Matthew was quite muscular, but after years of drinking and smoking, and smelling like an ashtray, it had taken its toll on his body. His fingers and teeth were yellow from the abuse. He now had long, lifeless, dark hair, down past his ears. He was six foot tall and starkly thin, and wore a dark tee shirt with no sleeves that had been worn many times and showed its age. His cut-off jeans were worn out and the flip-flops he wore on his feet, were slightly dirty as well as his ankles. He always had a beer can in his hand and was known to make moonshine in the woods behind his dilapidated house up on cinder blocks, at the edge of a forest conservation area.

His uncle had a large wooden vat on the ground behind the house, where he concocts his alcohol brew, or "juice" as he calls it, or his "moonshine elixir" "which would stupefy you with the fumes alone."

He was shiftless and too lazy to hold a regular job, and had no visible means of support. Sometimes, he would work with Zack's dad on some carpentry repair jobs, mostly as physical labor, carrying lumber or sheetrock.

Whatever he hunted, he'd sell to the locals. His wild meat and hides were popular, but the "elixirs" sold like crazy. It was a good thing he lived on the edge of the forest - should the deputy sheriff surprisingly show up, he could quietly vanish into the woods.

Zack had drunk some of his uncle's moonshine and said "It was smoother than velvet. It wasn't harsh and didn't burn your throat when swallowed."

They drove with the uncle in his big old white flat-bed truck to an area north of Sanford, to a tributary off the St. John River, then off-loaded the two canoes, the rifles and coolers. Zack placed the canoes in the water and told Adam to paddle with his uncle, and he would paddle with Sean.

After paddling for some time up the river, the uncle indicated a spot where the hogs had been tearing up the muddy riverbank. They pulled ashore and stepped out, immediately sinking into the mud, which kept sucking at their boots, while trudging up the riverbank with the rifles.

At the top of the slope, the uncle yells out, "Drop your rifles and climb the nearest tree boys - the sow is charging!"

The group all shimmied up the trees, each as thick as your thigh. Sean couldn't believe how fast Adam, with one arm in a sling from a basketball injury, was climbing his tree with one good arm and legs. He didn't know he was that strong. Climbing those rope rings in gym class gave him strength.

The sow for some reason, chose Adam's tree to work on. She grunted and squealed, using her tusks to root the base. None of us dared move. Zack's uncle kept yelling, "Don't be afraid. She can't knock it over."

"Oh yeah!", says Adam. "It's not your tree she's working on."

Finally, the sow moves off after an intense half hour of effort to bring these intruders down. She was huge, black, and she stank. With a grunt, she moved into the under-brush, with her piglets following her.

After a bit of time had passed, the uncle said, "Better get down now. Grab your rifles and run like hell to the canoes. She may be in wait, and will charge again."

You didn't have to tell them twice. They were down from the trees, heading for the canoes at breakneck speed. They slopped through the mud until Sean got stuck in a quicksand patch of mud, holding him down.

The uncle yells loudly again, "The sow is coming back. Hurry! Hurry! Get into the canoes!" Sean struggled to free his one foot from the mud which was up to his knees. He looked back at the sow coming over the embankment, seeing only her beady red eyes and tusks. The hog was making a sound that sounded like "Wheee Wheee". He screamed, and with a final thrust, pulled himself free and ran down the mud bank drunkenly and threw himself into the canoe, just as the sow hit the water with a splash.

Zack, by then, was back-paddling to the center of the tributary, with the bow facing upstream.

Sean was kneeling on the bottom of the canoe, head down, drooling with snot running down his chin. As the fear released its hold on him, he slowly lifted his head up to see his white knuckles holding the gunwales of the canoe.

He slowly crawled to the seat in the front of the canoe, and paddled as best he could, wiping the mess off his face with his arm.

After paddling for a while, Zack says, "I never heard you scream like that before."

Turning around angrily, Sean said, "You would too if a 350 pound pig was charging you. I've never been so scared in my life."

Zack just calmly paddled on. "I had my scares too", he

said. "I'll never forget how the hairs on the back of my neck stood up as I encountered a mama black bear with her cubs. I had to run and throw myself into a swampy area to get away from her. She felt I was a threat to her cubs, and charged." Then he yells, "Let's get out of here, and go up river to see what else is here, and drink our beer."

As they paddled, someone joked how brave they were, and "I'm not scared" came out of someone's mouth. It was all a bunch of crap, but who cares - they were safe now in the canoes.

Sean yells out, "Hey Adam, how's the arm?"

"A bit sore", he says.

"No, I mean the good one!" Their laughter could be heard through the casuarina pines as they disappeared around a bend in the river.

Chapter 34

Wild Turkey

The cell phone rang. It was Zack. "Sean get Adam, and meet me on the beach tonight. I have a surprise for you guys."

On the way over to the beach, Adam asked, "What's the surprise?"

"I don't know", Sean replied, as they came over the top of the sand dune, and saw Zack sitting with his nap-sack next to him.

It was a beautiful, clear night. The stars were visible, with a half moon illuminating the beach. On the horizon you could see the lights of the ships far out. Some fishermen in their boats were closer to shore, doing a bit of night fishing along the reefs.

"Hey Zack, what's up?", Adam asks.

Zack said, "Tonight we're going to be men." He reached into his nap-sack and pulled out a bottle of Wild Turkey whiskey, and pointed it up into the night sky. "Hell, this is my father's private stash. He'll never miss it. I've been sipping on it waiting for you guys. Tonight we will drink and be drunken sailors."

Adam asks, "Where did you find it?"

"My dad had it in the freezer. When I was putting my

wrapped meat in, I found the bottle behind some other frozen food. He'll never miss it", Zack says.

They passed the bottle around, making funny faces with each sip. After a few drinks, Adam stood up laughing. "I'm soooo drunk." he said, and started staggering like a drunk. Sean knew he wasn't - no one could get drunk that fast. They all played along with Adam pretending they were "bombed", staggered around, fell down and laughed so hard, that they had to take a piss. If anyone saw them, they'd think they were nuts, lined up at the surf's edge, peeing and laughing, to see who could pee the farthest - Adam won.

After this tomfoolery, they laid down on the sand with hands behind their heads, and looked up at the night sky. It was so quiet and peaceful. Nobody was around.

Zack began telling them about his life. "You know, my father is a drunk, and yells a lot, and has been doing this for most of his life. I knew very little about him when I grew up. My mother divorced him at a very young age, from all his verbal abuse, and arguments. When she couldn't take it anymore, she turned to drugs, and almost killed herself. She took very good care of me somehow. After a few tempestuous affairs, she decided to never marry, not even her boyfriend, whom we live with today. No wonder children are confused when their parents divorce and live with someone else. It's a lack of trust in God, and degrades the sanctity of marriage. Children should be raised in a healthy situation so that they have a greater chance of a successful marriage themselves. My mother's divorce has hardened her heart to remarriage. Maybe I can't blame her. The abusive words my father and she used towards each other, were not healthy or life giving. It will be hard to find forgiveness now.

The one good time I can remember while with my dad, was when I was ten years old. He took me flying in his crop duster airplane. It was painted yellow and blue. He surprised me with a leather helmet and goggles to wear, and off we flew into the blue. It was so much fun flying low over the fields and then swooping up and over the trees. After we turned the plane around and swooped down again, we pretended we were ace pilots from WWI, shooting our machine guns at the enemy below. I even handled the controls for a while. I really loved that day with him."

There was a long pause, then Zack said, "Hey, pass me that bottle. My mouth is dry."

Adam and Sean just laid there quietly, listening to Zack. They knew he just wanted to talk, and unburden himself from the lack of attention from his father, and possibly his mother too.

Chapter 35

Graduation

This would be their last spring together before they moved away and got on with their lives. Sean walked down to the Community Center, to watch Adam play basketball outside with some younger teenagers. He was still good, dashing here and there, running down the court and laying the basketball up into the hoop. The younger boys were in admiration of him.

Sean never told Zack about Adam's half year away. He figured he wouldn't understand. For that matter, neither did he, totally. He would never ask questions of Adam and how he felt now. It wasn't necessary. Besides, he doesn't know what to ask, without opening old wounds in him.

Maybe, it was the feeling of being disconnected from his adopted parents, who did love him, and gave him a secure life. Perhaps, it was not knowing his real parents - his heritage - no matter how good or bad it was.

Sean remembered reading a quote from J.B. Robb: "Heredity can be a strong pull. Heredity and early environment together, an almost irresistible pull."

Zack and Sean knew their parents. In Sean's case, it was his grandparents. Still, it's their family.

Adam wanted personal love; someone who would love only him. It's what he thought about, sitting up in the bleachers watching him play a good basketball game.

When the game was over, Adam came over to Sean, toweling himself off, and commented how good it felt playing ball again.

"Hey Adam", Sean said. "Big party tonight. Want to go?"

"Booze and broads?", Adam asks.

"What do you think? Zack will be there and wants us to check things out."

"Okay, I'm game. See ya tonight", Adam said.

The party was noisy. Buckets of cold beer were on ice, as well as sodas, and bags of chips and salsa nearby. Music was playing. Zack was with the girls talking a "blue streak."

Adam found some girls he knew, and was talking and "toasting his beer" with them.

Sean could see he was happy and excited. Adam asked one of the girls to dance. Sean noticed the girl had eyes only for him.

Adam passed the required tests that semester in high school, and would graduate with the senior class. Sean was happy that the three of them would be in this together.

After the graduation ceremonies, everyone gathered outside the school's auditorium. Adam brought his parents, the Rymans, to be introduced to Sean's grandparents and Uncle Preston. Then Zack came over with his mom and her boyfriend. Zack was a head taller than his mom. She was proud of him and kept looking up at him with admiration. Sean realized how much Zack looked like the Olympic gold medal swimmer, Phelps - tall, dark curly hair, big hands and strength. "Oh, the girls are going to love him", he thought.

"Hey, Zack", he asked. "What are you going to do now?"

"I'm joining the Army. I want to build bombs and blow up things and get the aggression out of me."

"Okay", he says. "What about you Adam? Any plans?"

"I'm not sure yet, but it has to be something technical", he said. "What are you going to do?", Adam asks of Sean.

"College - something local. I've already been accepted to Rollins College in Orlando. I want to stay in Florida.", he answers.

They embrace each other, hands on their shoulders, and touch their foreheads together with their graduation caps on.

"Ya know guys, I love you. Peace and wisdom", Sean says. "It's been some run together. The era is over. Let's stay in touch, okay?"

"Okay", they say.

As they walk away from each other with their families, Sean yells out once again, "Guys, don't forget! Stay in touch!", giving them a farewell salute with two fingers off his cap.

Chapter 36

Park Ave.

I t's four years later. He had never been here before. In all the years of living in Florida, he had never walked Park Avenue in Winter Park, north of Orlando.

His car was parked at the beginning of the street, near the decorated thick columns at the entrance to Rollins College, a private liberal arts college. The campus is tree lined with huge old oak trees and camphor trees. There are also soaring palms and pines and camellia bushes so big they look like trees. The college itself is designed in the Mediterranean style on the shore of Lake Virginia, where scenic boat rides are offered. All the streets are brick paved, as well as Park Avenue.

He walked the street, observing the students walking around in small groups. The were all clean cut and well dressed in their shorts and shirts. He did see some college girls showing their cheeks below their shorts. "Why do girls do this? Are they giving some sort of 'come on' to the boys? No wonder some of them get in trouble or harassed", he thought.

He continued walking, seeing all the shops beckoning him to come in. There was a wide range of restaurants available on both sides of the street with their brightly colored tables and chairs, inviting you to dine. A museum with a collection of Tiffany's art and a huge Catholic Church, St. Mary Magdalen, was at the end of his walk.

The street is quieter and more sophisticated than most walkable streets of Florida. It served the college students well with its hamburger and pizza joints. The higher class, gentry groups of shoppers with higher tastes had shops like William-Sonoma, Pottery Barn, Lilly Pulitzer, as well as art galleries, coffee houses, a Chocolatier, a wine room and a cigar shop. There's even a small theater and fitness center. No one was in there at the moment when he looked in.

As he walked by the big store windows, he noticed how he looked. His hair was disheveled and his clothes were worn, not as handsome as he once was, with his long blonde hair, years ago.

He walked by the Park Plaza Hotel, and looked in the window at the diners in the restaurant. It was an historic building, and known for its excellent dining room and huge crystal chandelier. A waiter, a young man in his twenties was serving a couple of diners, wearing a crisp white shirt and black bow tie. He looked familiar. From where? So he entered the restaurant and asked the hostess who that waiter was. She said, "Sean."

"What time does he get off work?", he asked

"About five o'clock."

"Thank you." he said, and left. Later, he went around back to the parking lot of the restaurant, and waited for Sean to come out. He sat on the grass under the shade of a big Canary Island date palm, and looked around. The parking lot had two rows of the palms on grass islands, with the cars parked up next to them.

Soon Sean came out the back door from under the black canopy shading the exit, and went to his car. That's when he made his move.

"Hello Sean", he said.

Sean was startled at that moment, trying to figure out who this guy was. "Do I know you?", he asked.

"Yes, it's Lance."

"Get away from me. I don't want any part of you as a friend." Sean said.

Sean had put on some weight, and was older, of course, and had a clean cut hair style. He just glared at Lance.

Lance said, "Look, I'm not here to harm you. I just want to say how sorry I am for what I did to you in high school."

"Why?", asked Sean.

"Well I have hepatitis C and there's no cure at the moment for it. I'm sick and slowly dying. My minister says I have to make restitution for all those I've injured in the past few years. When I saw you waiting on those diners, I just had to wait and say how sorry I am once again. I've lost my looks, and money. I can't seem to keep a job. I'm a mess. I had a fairly wild life after high school, messing with injected drugs and sex. Now, I'm paying the price. I just didn't take care of myself during this time."

"Look Lance, you emasculated me. I suffered for a few years after what you and your buddies did to me. I was an innocent kid who didn't know anything. I trusted people and you took that all away from me. I just wished you had come over and said how sorry you were at the time. Maybe I could have felt better about myself. Maybe I wouldn't have had to keep my rape a secret. You would ignore me in the hallway when passing by with your tennis buddies. You made me feel like a piece of crap, like I was nothing, a nobody", said Sean.

"Sean, you're so right. I'm the piece of crap now and I will pay for it. Please accept my apology. Forget about me. Get on with your life. You have a bright future", Lance said.

Sean asks "What happened to Casper and that other guy?"

"Casper disappeared after high school, like a ghost. He

really didn't want any part of what we did to you. It bothered him tremendously. He never mentioned it again. As for the other guy, he was kind of wild like me. He got into a terrible car accident and was paralyzed from the waist down", said Lance.

"I would never wish on another man what you have. It's a terrible price to pay for your indiscretions. I wish you the best Lance, and I hope I never see you again", said Sean.

Sean got into his blue compact car, backed up, and drove out of the parking lot and headed for home. His apartment is small - few blocks from Uncle Preston. He'll finish his last year at Rollins College with a degree in English and a minor in writing. Grandma had saved his parents' life insurance money to put him through college. "I'm so thankful for that", he thought.

Zack called. He's in North Carolina working at the Army's Weapon Arsenal, making weapons. He met a girl from the local church. "This is the one", he said. He probably will marry her, have a slew of kids, teach them the way of the woods, and love them harder than his dad did with him.

As for Adam, he's in central California, wearing a white lab coat, trying to find out how to levitate toys. Once his company knows the principle, they will levitate cars. He lives in a yurt on a platform he built at the base of the mountains. During the winters, when the snow was on the land, he has to live in town with some friends, so that he won't freeze to death if he gets snowed in. He's doing fine and is still trying to discover himself.

"Me, I just want to graduate from college, marry a girl and get a good job here in Florida, which I still find so magical." As he is driving home, he thinks, "Isn't life wonderful."

Printed in the United States
By Bookmasters